DREAMING OF HIS SNOWED IN KISS

Cowboy Mountain Christmas
Book 4

JESSIE GUSSMAN

Contents

Acknowledgments

Cover art by Lara Wynter
Editing by Heather Hayden
Narration by Jay Dyess
Author Services by CE Author Assistant

Listen to the unabridged audio for FREE performed by Jay Dyess on the Say with Jay channel on YouTube. Get early access to all of Jay's recordings and listen to Jessie's books before they're available to the general public, plus get daily Bible readings by Jay and bonus scenes by becoming a Say with Jay channel member.

I love my newsletter. I have the best readers in the world. They constantly amaze me with their comments and stories and thoughts. It's a real blessing to me to get to be on the receiving end of words that truly move me. I love sharing them.

The idea for this book came from one of my readers. I had asked in my newsletter for readers to send me stories of their best, favorite or most memorable Christmas.

One of my subs sent me the story of a Christmas they had that wasn't at Christmas. It was such a beautiful story of a family's love that I knew I had to use it. I was given permission and this book is the result.

I want to dedicate this story to her, to her beautiful family and to the last "Christmas" they all spent together.

Chapter One

*P*oppy Kyle slowed her car to a crawl and gave the old rickety bridge a second look.

She wasn't a naturally positive person, but she'd worked hard the last few years to train herself to always see the good.

Most of the time, it worked.

She bit her lip as her finger tapped on the steering wheel. Positive thinking wasn't helping her to see this bridge in any light other than rotted and old and about to fall into the admittedly placid-looking river below.

The river wasn't exceptionally wide or deep, and the bridge wasn't terribly high; still, maybe it was conditioning since childhood, or maybe it was just a natural inclination, but the idea of falling into it as the bridge collapsed made her keep her foot on the brake and her finger tapping on the wheel.

She lifted her eyes. West Barclay's house and barn were two hundred yards on the other side of the river.

She could smell the steaming meatloaf and almost taste the mashed potatoes that were packed in newspaper and sitting in a box in the back of her car along with three other casseroles that could be frozen or cooked later this week.

She supposed Pastor Race and Miss Penny would be extremely disappointed in her if someone were to find her parked alongside the road, halfway back to town, with the meatloaf and mashed potatoes half gone and crumbs in her lap.

Her stomach rumbled, almost as though putting up an argument in favor of losing her position at the church.

Even if it was volunteer, the idea of not being dependable didn't sit right.

She shoved the idea out of her head, less appealing for the food aspect, maybe, than for the idea of not having to drive over that bridge.

Her finger hadn't stopped tapping. She leaned forward, looking up at the sky, like that would help anything.

She kept hearing about a "storm of the century" coming. Next week. But in her experience, the weather station liked to exaggerate things. They went wild and crazy with their green crayon any time it rained and even wilder and crazier with the white one when it was time to snow.

Not that Arkansas saw that much snow.

But she hadn't always lived in Arkansas.

She sighed. The sky hadn't given her any answers, not that she expected them. Looking out through the windshield, she scanned the picturesque Ozark Mountains that created the backdrop behind West's house.

Pretty.

Beautiful, actually.

Although she hated to give West Barclay any more credit than he deserved. Or his house.

He treated her like an annoying insect—a gnat flying around his head. One he put up with but would prefer to swat away.

Her brain wanted to get stuck on that track, but she pulled it back.

Positive thinking.

Anyway, regardless of how West treated her, he was in over his head with his new houseguest and her four children. Which was why Poppy had a car full of food for them.

Unfortunately, her car was on this side of the creek. In order to get on the side of the creek where West, his guest, her children, and his house was, she had to cross that rickety old bridge.

Tempted to get out and visually inspect the bridge, she stopped with her hand on the latch.

What would a visual inspection help? She wasn't an engineer.

Even an engineer couldn't predict with infallibility whether or not the bridge was going to collapse.

Maybe she'd be better off to say a prayer and have faith.

Lord? Am I supposed to die today? Maybe You could let me deliver the food first?

Holy smokes. She hadn't even thought of that. She'd have to cross the bridge twice. Once on the way over, and once on the way back.

Consider West's pickup.

Maybe it wasn't the Lord speaking to her—He should be talking about lilies of the field rather than pickups—but it was definitely a voice of reason.

His pickup was much bigger, and she assumed much heavier, than her little compact car. Probably it would be an accurate assumption that if the bridge could hold his pickup, it could hold her car too.

Maybe it was the prayer, maybe it was the voice of reason—although she truly believed that God was reasonable and she did not find reason and prayer mutually exclusive—she felt her foot lifting off the brake pedal and sliding slowly to the gas.

She wasn't exactly an expert on driving, and she was kind of torn. Should she go slow and stay on the bridge longer, causing less trauma with the slower speed? Or should she go as fast as she could, taking the chance that she might hit a bump and come down hard with the bouncing, giving undue pressure on what looked like old, rotted timbers?

Deciding moderation was always a good choice, she closed her eyes and pressed on the pedal.

Wait a second. Old rickety bridge or no, she was almost begging for trouble to drive with her eyes closed. They snapped back open.

She laughed at herself.

She trained herself to be happy, yes, but she hadn't completely conquered the common sense she'd been born without.

What seemed reasonable and obvious to everyone else seemed like a brilliant discovery to her, years after other people had figured things out.

Like driving with their eyes open.

She knew it; she just forgot sometimes.

Her front tires hit the old timbers of the bridge and began to rumble across.

The thought that she could point the steering wheel straight and still close her eyes tugged hard at the back of her mind, but she kept her lids up. She would be brave.

She could be both happy and brave.

Maybe having problems to work out was good for her. Always in the back of her mind was the knowledge that she could end up like her mother. After all, she'd gone through the same horrifying experience.

Just because she hadn't fallen into a deep depression right away didn't mean it couldn't happen.

She wouldn't let it.

It felt like years before her front tires hit solid ground on the other side, and she let out the breath she was holding. The food had made it safely across, and so had she.

Now all she had to do was go back over the bridge on her way home.

It didn't take any time at all to pull up to the house and grab the hot food. She'd come back for the casseroles in a bit. It was February, just a few days before Valentine's Day, and even though it was Arkansas, it wasn't hot.

As she climbed the porch to the small house, she realized with the pan of food in each hand, she wasn't going to be able to knock on the door.

What sounded like a muffled thump and a scream on the other side of the door made her wonder about the wisdom of whether this was a good time.

If they wanted their food hot, it had to be a good time. Also, she really didn't want to have to drive over the bridge three more times instead of one, so she was going to deliver it right now despite any inconvenience.

Another three thumps in quick succession had her pulling her lip in and biting down on it. It sounded like maybe the kids had taken over in there.

Maybe she could help.

For the woman and her kids who were staying here and not necessarily for West.

Using her elbow, she rang the doorbell, hoping it worked.

She couldn't hear whether it rang or not.

It felt like forever that she stood waiting before using her elbow to ring again.

She'd given up and was looking for a place to put the pans in her hands down so she could knock when the door jerked open.

West, with a screaming baby in one arm and a crying child holding onto his left leg, stood facing her.

Poppy had been a Christian all her life. She'd been taught not to laugh at another's calamity. That seeing someone else suffering shouldn't make her smile. That she should love everyone and not wish ill on anyone.

Maybe she was arrogant, but she thought, usually, she did a pretty good job on those.

Still, seeing West so overwhelmed with the crying baby and the clinging toddler and the yelling that was going on behind him, she couldn't help it.

She smirked.

"I'd really like to send you away, because I don't want to see happy people right now, but if you're holding food, you can come in." West's eyes had narrowed, and while his words, spoken above the crying child, were not terribly kind, they did represent the type of relationship that she seemed to have with him.

Not hateful; they didn't hate each other. But not friendly either. Kind of a jabbing, poking relationship.

Her smirk fell right in line with that, and his annoyance at her happiness was typical as well.

Apparently, West preferred to be around sour, grumpy people all the time.

She wasn't going to go back and undo all the work she'd done just to keep West happy.

Plus, she highly suspected that he wouldn't be happy anyway, no matter what she did.

He said he picked on her because she was like Pollyanna, but she thought it was her in particular, and not happiness in general, that he didn't like.

"It's hot. You can eat it right now."

He stood back, allowing her plenty of space to pass and saying without words that she was welcome to come in as long as she stayed away from him.

Not a problem.

She walked past and stood in the living room, looking around and trying to figure out which direction to go to get to the kitchen, as the door clicked closed behind her.

She looked over her shoulder as West scooped the child that was clinging to his leg up in his other arm while trying to bounce the baby in his right.

"Follow me," he said, not unkindly but not necessarily friendly either.

There were a couple of trucks and some kitchen utensils scattered through the living room as he walked past, taking a right and walking into the kitchen. No sign of the woman whose children they were, but the two small children that he wasn't holding stood back against the wall, wide-eyed and staring at her, a stranger, walking in.

Her heart tore at their forlorn expressions.

"How's their mother doing?" she asked, raising her voice to be heard above the crying baby.

"Not good," West said matter-of-factly, turning and looking around at her as he said it, his face not giving away anything.

He had to be sad. She was sure he was, but he was definitely the kind of person that was not comfortable sharing his feelings. Happy or sad.

"You can set them on the counter."

Poppy did, and then she turned, intending to tell him she had more casseroles in the car that she would carry in.

But her eyes hooked on the child in his arms. Not the baby who was still crying, but the little one who had been clinging to his leg. He had one dirty pudgy fist stuck in his mouth and was chewing on it like a nervous habit, which sent a pang through her chest that a one-year-old would even have a nervous habit. His other pudgy fist rubbed his eye like it was past his nap time.

Poppy didn't have children of her own, but she'd spent plenty of time in church nurseries, among other things, and had a lot of experience with young ones.

She lowered her head a little, so she wasn't looking at the child head-on—that seemed to be less intimidating in her experience. Then she smiled, not a full, big smile showing lots of teeth. That, too, seemed to intimidate small children. Just a little smile, and she ducked her head even more.

"Are you hungry?" she asked in a soft, sweet voice.

The child looked at her suspiciously, and then West's eyes

opened wide as the little boy took his fist out of his mouth and leaned his whole body toward her.

She didn't bother to look at West to ask permission. They'd spent enough time in church and various activities bantering with each other that she felt comfortable with him, even if she didn't think he liked her too much.

He wasn't going to deny her taking a crying, fussing child out of his hand.

"It looks like it's nap time for him?"

"Past," he said shortly.

"Garrett pooped his pants."

Poppy blinked and looked at the doorway where a serious, sober-faced boy with what appeared to be dried egg on his cheek stood staring at her.

She nodded. Okay. He seemed to consider that important information. She would too.

"Was that just now?"

The little boy shook his head at the same time West answered.

"No, I think Warren is saying that's why we don't have Gabriella down for her nap. Or fed. Because there was something more pressing that I needed to take care of than a screaming baby. Not that I would have thought that were possible."

"Of course. Poop. Or fire." She refused to allow the shudder that went through her to pull her thoughts in the direction they wanted to go. "A fire would be the only other thing that would be more pressing than a screaming baby."

Poppy slanted her eyes at West, only half kidding. She'd never been able to exactly joke about what happened to her, but she wasn't going to allow it to cloud her life. It would throw her into such a deep, dark depression she would never emerge.

Like her mother.

West snapped his fingers and pointed. "I hadn't thought of that. But you're right. Fire would be worse." He seemed to think for a second. "*In* the house fire. *Out* of the house fire, not more urgent."

"Yeah. We could let the barn be burned down. As long as there aren't any animals in it."

"There are. But unless I could find someone to watch the children, I wouldn't take that chance."

Okay, she didn't like the idea that someone would have to choose between saving the life of an animal and saving the life of a child, but she did agree that the children were more important.

"You take care of her." She nodded at the baby, who must be a girl, even though she had a blue sleeper on. "And I'll feed these guys. If that will help."

West eyed her. He didn't look relieved exactly, almost skeptical, maybe.

Yeah. Their relationship hadn't exactly been super friendly.

Not her fault, Poppy told herself.

"Appreciate it," West said eventually, holding the baby in the crook of his arm as he rooted through the cupboard, she assumed looking for a container of baby formula since she saw the old one lying at the top of the overflowing trash can.

"All right, boys," she said, drawing out the word "boys." She was pretty sure from what she'd heard at church there were three boys plus the baby. "Let's get our hands washed, and we can sit down and have some lunch." She made a goofy face at the boy in her arms. "You guys hungry? I have mashed potatoes." She said "mashed potatoes" the way she might have said candy bars, because in her experience, kids love mashed potatoes.

The one in her arms stared at her along with the older boy West had called Warren.

This might be harder than she was expecting.

Chapter Two

West set the can of formula down on the counter and struggled to open it with one hand while trying to awkwardly bounce the screaming baby in his other arm.

Trying to be happy Poppy was there.

Actually, there was a lot of him that was happy that Poppy was there.

He did a good job of pretending she was annoying, but her bright face and happy personality lit up any room that she was in. And drew people like magnets. Him included.

She already had enough admirers. She didn't need him.

Still, that he was in over his head with these kids was obvious. And Minnie wasn't going to be getting out of bed anytime soon.

He'd heard her coughing last night. She was so weak and thin it amazed him that she was even able to get up at all.

He didn't want to be happy about the fact that the boys didn't jump when Poppy said "let's eat."

It was more of a struggle than what she was expecting, he was sure, to get their hands washed and their faces wiped and have them sitting down at the table.

He didn't smirk over that, either. After all, she was helping him.

By that time, he had managed to one-hand the formula container and mix up a bottle.

Gabriella still wasn't entirely convinced that bottles were better than her mother, but she was taking it better than she had five days ago. Thankfully.

Unfortunately, he didn't think her mother would ever be feeding her again.

Minnie knew it. Which is probably why she'd ended up at his house.

With a bottle in Gabriella's mouth and her blissfully sucking in sweet silence, he strode casually behind the chairs at the kitchen table where the little towheaded boys sat.

Trevor was strapped in the high chair.

The brand-new high chair that his bachelor's house had never seen the likes of, not until four days ago when Pastor Race had brought it.

Funny how he'd gone from totally inept with that chair to being able to put a kid in it one-handed in the last four days.

He couldn't believe two people could be alone at home with a houseful of children and actually raise them themselves.

The title of that book—*It Takes a Village*—made a lot more sense now. Obviously, the author was talking about how many people it took to feed two kids lunch and get up with a baby at night. He needed to assign about three people per child in order to keep up with everything.

"Do you want me to feed her while you eat?" Poppy asked.

Like his stomach heard the question, it growled right as Poppy asked.

"No, thank you."

He supposed he made fun of her perpetually happy personality because he felt threatened by it.

He had never thought of himself as a particularly dark person until his parents had died and he ended up in the same foster home as Minnie.

There'd been some goth, and Satan worshiping going on, along with a lot of other things that still felt heavy in his heart and soul. They were the kind of things a person couldn't shed just because they had a new home and a new life.

Poppy's sunshine threatened the dark corners of his heart.

Poppy drew his gaze as she slipped a spoonful of mashed potatoes into Trevor's mouth. He ate, but his eyes were big and shifted from her to West and back again.

Poor kid didn't understand why his mom was no longer taking care of him and why he wasn't someplace familiar and beloved.

He was too little to have things explained to him, and even Garrett, who—at three—seemed to understand, didn't take it easier.

He still cried every night. Sometimes, he cried in the afternoon, too.

The food smelled good though, and West figured he might as well sit down with the kids and try to make it seem at least a little normal. He wasn't sure exactly what was going to happen to the kids if or, more likely, when Minnie lost her cancer fight, and he'd been up to his eyeballs in trying to catch up to the kids and hadn't had a chance to talk to Minnie about it anyway.

Not that he wanted to bring it up.

"It must have been quite a surprise for you to see Minnie and her four children at church last Sunday," Poppy said, grinning, of course, and seeming to just want to make conversation.

He could adult. Really.

"It was. I think it would be a surprise for anyone."

"Are any of these children yours?" Poppy asked, just as casually, spooning more mashed potatoes into Trevor's mouth.

West's mouth dropped.

Of course, that was what people probably thought.

"No."

Poppy's eyes slipped to his, like she didn't quite believe him and was checking his face to make sure he wasn't messing with her.

"It seems odd that she would go to you, then? She's not your sister, is she?"

Now her questions were probing instead of making conversation, but he supposed these were questions everyone had. Questions that should be answered.

"After my parents were killed in a car accident, my siblings and I were split up and put in foster care. Minnie was in the house I was sent to." And that's all he was gonna say about that. To Poppy anyway. Someone as cute and sweet as her wouldn't understand the things he'd gone through. The things he'd done.

Poppy jerked her head in acknowledgment of his words. Then her face crumpled up a little bit as she asked softly, "How is she?"

He shook his head. She wasn't good. "She has a doctor's appointment tomorrow. I guess we'll know better then."

They didn't talk any more throughout lunch, as Poppy fed the baby and didn't say anything.

West ate. He was hungry, and he didn't resent her help exactly. Just didn't always appreciate her constant smile and happy attitude.

"I want to go outside and play," Warren said as he scraped his plate.

"Do you want something more to eat?" Poppy asked, ignoring his statement.

Gabriella had finished her bottle, which West had managed to hold with one hand while eating with the other, and he pulled it out of her mouth, taking his napkin and putting it on his shoulder for a burp rag.

In his experience, he needed one. Unless he wanted to change his clothes.

The other option was smelling like baby puke for the rest of the day.

That had happened.

Twice.

Then he'd gotten smart.

The napkin wasn't guaranteed to keep that from happening, but he couldn't remember where he'd put the last burp rag, and he wasn't going looking for it right now. If this was going to be a longtime thing, he needed to get more organized.

It wasn't going to be a longtime thing.

"Once everyone's done eating, we'll put Trevor and Garrett to bed, and you and I can go outside for a bit, okay, bud?"

Warren chewed on his lip. "What about Gabby?"

West couldn't help it; one side of his mouth pulled back.

He'd said the same thing to Warren yesterday after lunch, only Gabby hadn't gone down for a nap, so he'd ended up spending the afternoon inside, and he and Warren hadn't made it out.

In fact, his stock hadn't gotten fed or checked until after he'd managed to get everybody down for the night last night, which had been late.

"Hopefully, she'll go to sleep, too." He didn't know what else to say. He couldn't hardly go outside and carry a baby and work at the same time. He didn't have anything to put her in. Like a buggy or whatever they called things like that nowadays.

"I could put the kids down for now and watch the baby, if you don't mind carrying the food in from the car before you go out and do your work." Poppy's never-ending smile was on her face, and she spoke without looking at him.

Instead, she made a face at Garrett and got him to grin.

West didn't say anything, though, and he resented the appreciation he felt for her. He didn't want to start to like her.

"I can stay for a while, if it'll help you." She turned to him, her smile just as big as it always was. He didn't let himself smile back.

"If you get the kids down, you can tell Minnie to call me if she needs me, and then you can go. I'd appreciate it."

"Will she be awake? Would she like some food?" Poppy looked around, like she supposed that Minnie had been sleeping and now realized she'd neglected her duty by not fixing her a plate.

In West's experience, Minnie wasn't going to eat anything anyway. Maybe a few bites.

"She's upstairs in the first bedroom on the left." Gabriella let out a deep burp. It never failed to surprise West that such a small baby could make such a loud noise.

"I can take her. You can go." Poppy stood, holding her hands for the baby.

West definitely wasn't going to fight about it.

He held Gabby out to Poppy. The little body felt warm and light and cuddly, and his arms felt strangely light as Poppy lifted her out of his hands.

He reminded himself he'd have plenty of time with her at night, when she seemed to spend most of the hours screaming and stiff as a board.

Still, it was almost impossible not to fall completely in love with her, helpless and fatherless.

The urge to buy her something pink also surprised him.

Minnie had explained that all she had were boys' clothes, and she hadn't been shopping since Gabriella had been born.

West helped clear off the table, and then as Poppy held Gabriella in one hand and Trevor's hand in the other, she left the room while chatting with Garrett, taking the children upstairs.

"I guess it's just you and me, bud," he said to Warren.

"I want to go outside."

He nodded. "Let's get these dishes in the dishwasher, then we'll do that."

Chapter Three

oppy cradled the tiny little body of Gabriella in her arms. The little one couldn't be more than a month or two old. If that.

Her little rosebud mouth pursed as she blew her breath out, her eyelashes peacefully resting on her chubby little baby cheeks, and her body completely limp. Trusting.

Pain, dull now instead of sharp, pushed through Poppy's chest, and she remembered another baby, from another time, time that felt like ages ago, who had been just as trusting and just as precious.

She shook her head, willing the memories to go away and putting the smile that she'd worked so hard to have back on her face again.

She would not have children; she'd already made that decision because she didn't think she could fight this feeling every day.

But that didn't mean she couldn't love other peoples' kids.

Especially babies.

She'd already put Trevor and Garrett down and seen the crib in the darkened corner of the bedroom on the left, since the door had been cracked.

She'd also seen the still form on the bed. She assumed that was Minnie.

She hadn't talked to Minnie since she'd come to West's home, although the church had delivered other meals.

Poppy was in charge of the benevolence ministries, and she'd coordinated the meals, but this was the first one she'd delivered.

Slipping the door open just enough for her to glide through, she tiptoed into the room, intending to set Gabriella down and tiptoe right back out.

The room had that stale smell of a sickroom, which almost drowned out the now-familiar male scent that was uniquely West's. She didn't see any of his stuff lying around, but from the scent, she assumed he'd given up his bedroom for Minnie.

Again, she wondered what Minnie was to him, not that she cared.

There was definitely something odd about the feeling that she had for West, but so far, she'd been successful in terming it antagonism. The kind that two people had who would never be able to get along but were too much adults to actually fight.

Whether she was just deluding herself about that or not, she wasn't sure.

She'd never had feelings like that for anyone else.

The kind of feelings where she couldn't wait to see him and couldn't wait to get away from him. Not exactly the kind of feeling she'd ever had for anyone else.

Definitely confusing.

The form on the bed didn't move as she slipped closer to the crib, the baby stirring in her hands just slightly. She adjusted the warm body, getting ready to lay her down.

Her own mother and little sister were somewhere in northern Arkansas right now.

The guilt that she could never quite shake tightened her neck as she thought that maybe rather than helping Race and Penny, she should be back with her mother and Hazel.

She had to live her life, and her mother wanted to stay stuck in the past.

Or maybe she was just afraid that what her mother had would be contagious.

There were things she didn't want to think about, so she shook those thoughts off as well, gently setting Gabriella down in the crib and tucking the blanket around her.

The baby stirred and jerked as babies do before settling back and relaxing.

In the dim light, Poppy could just make out her outline, and she smiled at it. Precious little one.

Turning, she took two steps before a voice came softly and weakly in the darkness. "Who is that?"

Poppy swallowed. In the year or so that she'd been with Race and Penny and in the years before that with her parents, she'd been around a lot of people who were sick and tired and had given up hope. Her mother being one.

She was never sure what to say to these people. Her own journey was so long and so hard she couldn't sum it up into a sentence or two that might be coherent, and sometimes, she just felt it wouldn't help anyway.

All of her problems had been in her mind.

It wasn't like she had cancer, with her body being slowly eaten away and death creeping closer and more certain every day.

She wasn't sure the foundation she'd built in her mind would handle that kind of load. "It's Poppy Kyle. I work with the church in Mistletoe, and I brought some food out for you and your children."

"And West."

Poppy nodded, although she realized Minnie probably couldn't see her, so she said softly, "Yes. And West."

"He's grown up into a good man."

Poppy nodded again. Unsure what else to say. She didn't know West when he was younger.

"But he's bitter and angry, and he needs to let the past go."

Again, Poppy didn't know anything about West's past, although Minnie's words made guilt tighten her neck and travel down her backbone. She hadn't thought that West might have gone through anything hard. She had trouble cutting people slack when their trials hadn't been as severe as hers.

Maybe she was arrogant, thinking she had it worse than anyone else, and if she could live through it, everyone else should be able to too.

God gave different trials to different people.

"I'm sorry I woke you up," she whispered, bending over just a little and finding Minnie's hand on the bed with her own, grabbing it and squeezing. How difficult it must be to have four children who needed you and be unable to get out of bed to take care of them.

Minnie seemed to squint into the darkness at Poppy, and then she said, "I think it will be good for him."

Poppy didn't say anything. She didn't want to talk about West. She had no idea how to define her feelings for him. She couldn't talk to a stranger about them when she didn't even know what they were herself.

"I thought..." Minnie's voice trailed off for a moment. "I thought, once upon a time, there could be something between him and me, but I think we were too much alike. He needs someone who hasn't suffered like he has. Who doesn't have the same darkness in their soul, and whose smile can light up a room along with the dark cracks of his heart."

The slender hand under hers moved, squeezing Poppy's fingers weakly. "I remember seeing you on the church steps. Your smile and your energy and the compassion that just seems to flow from you was enough to touch my soul. I wish I could be like that. But I think that's what West needs."

Minnie was so wrong. She had no idea how wrong she was. For maybe the thousandth time, Poppy wondered if people actually knew what had happened to her whether they would think that her smile was just a fake covering.

It wasn't. Maybe it had been at first, but the joy of the Lord truly *was* her strength.

It wasn't something that happened without a conscious effort on her part, though. Because it was much easier to give in to the darkness.

How to explain that to Minnie?

"Are you feeling okay?" she asked instead, not wanting to explain her past and not wanting to talk about West at all.

"I'm dying," Minnie said matter-of-factly, although her voice was still reedy and thin.

"I'm sorry." What else was there to say?

"Not your fault. Everyone does it at some point."

"Aren't you scared?" Poppy couldn't help the words that came out.

Fear was part of the motivation she'd had for grabbing joy with both hands and wrapping it around her like a cloak.

"Not for me. At first, yes. Definitely. But now, I can't wait to get to heaven. I hurt all the time. It's getting worse. Except..." Her head turned toward the crib, and her hand clutched, feebly, at Poppy's. "Until I think of my children. And then, the pain in my body is nothing. Not compared to the pain that's in my heart."

Poppy could understand that a little, because of what she'd been through. Although she hadn't left her children. On the contrary, her siblings had been taken from her. A difference, sure, but a parting nonetheless.

Her mother had lost her children.

And Poppy had lost her mother, even though she was still here.

"You don't have to stay. I'm awake. If Gabriella cries, I can get her."

"Are you sure?"

"Yes. Usually, the afternoon is my best time. I'll be fine. Where's West?"

"He went outside with Warren."

Minnie's head moved in a semblance of a nod on her pillow. "I should have put Warren in school. He's old enough." Her chin trembled. "This is hard enough for him, and he was having a hard time adjusting. I didn't want to add the school adjustment on top of everything."

"Sometimes, that gives a schedule and stability," Poppy said, although she didn't disagree with Minnie's decision.

"If it weren't all new, I would agree. But kindergarten is a big adjustment anyway. It would have been too much with the move and everything."

"No one knows a child like their mother."

Rather than comforting, her words seemed to make Minnie melt even more into the mattress. Poppy could have kicked herself. She was just reminding Minnie that she wasn't going to be there to raise her children.

"I'm sorry. That was inconsiderate."

"No. It's not your fault. You don't have to trip over yourself to try not to offend me. People get offended way too easily."

"I'll try to be more careful."

"Does that mean you're coming back?"

"Probably. Do you want me to stop in and see you?"

"Please. Just a short visit. Anything else wears me out."

"I'll be back," Poppy said softly as she squeezed Minnie's hand one last time and backed away. She was curious as to how Minnie had such a young baby and yet was obviously dying. She was also curious about her connection to West. Although she shouldn't be. And even more curious about the baby's father and what would happen to the children if Minnie was indeed, as she said, dying.

"I look forward to seeing you," Minnie said softly as her hand slipped out of Poppy's and fell back to the bed.

Chapter Four

"Garrett has to pee," Warren said with the wisdom of an older brother as they walked into Mistletoe's diner after dropping Minnie off at her doctor's appointment.

Penny had offered to go in with her. So West had an hour or so to kill with the kids.

Since they'd run out of the house without eating, he figured he'd better feed them. Although it probably would have been better to take them to the park. The entire winter, they'd had milder than usual temperatures, and today was following that trend.

Still, the kids needed to eat, and there were no fast-food restaurants in Mistletoe.

"We'll go straight to the bathrooms," West said, knowing from experience when Garrett had to pee, it was an immediate thing. There wasn't too much of a window between the warning and when the actual event began

Christmas bells jingled above his head, and despite the fact it was almost Valentine's Day, Christmas music played over the speakers. Christmas music played year-round at Mistletoe Diner. The Christmas trees in the corner that never came down were decorated with hearts. The town of Mistletoe didn't know there was any season other than Christmas.

With the baby carrier in one hand, he held Trevor with the other and the door with his foot as Garrett and Warren slipped by into the restaurant. He shouldn't have had the opportunity to see that Poppy was standing at a table, notepad in hand, apron tied around her slender waist, and that perpetual smile that he could see even though she was in profile to him lighting up the world around her.

It was almost enough to make him want to turn around and go right back out, despite the fact that he was having a bathroom emergency with one of the kids.

Her eyes glanced toward him at the sound of the bells, and he wasn't sure what the double take that she did meant. Then her eyes swept over all the kids and back to him before she focused her attention on the table in front of her.

He nodded at her, which she acknowledged with a jerk of her chin. Nothing more.

Man, he hated this feeling. The feeling of wanting to be away from her, wanting to be closer to her. The buzz of excitement of seeing her, along with the nervousness that he could do without if she weren't here. But the idea of not seeing her was too disappointing, and he couldn't wish for that.

He hated those tied up and unable to figure them out feelings.

He hated feelings in general. And would honestly prefer not to have any.

He definitely wasn't going to think about them.

"Go on, boys. Straight ahead." Thankfully, the restrooms weren't hard to get to. He didn't know what else to do with Gabriella except take her in with him and set her on the floor.

Minnie had mentioned changing stations, but they must have been a ladies' restroom thing.

It made him think of a big table, with piles of diapers and wipes and soft cushions for babies' heads and maybe even some kind of mobile dangling above their eyes to keep them from crying, which seemed to be the automatic reaction to a baby getting her diaper changed.

At least that was Gabriella's reaction.

Maybe because the poor thing hadn't had any stability in her young life, although after talking to Minnie just a bit more, he knew Gabriella would have a beautiful story to tell people when she grew older about how her mother had sacrificed her life for Gabriella's.

She might not know her mother, ever, but she would know for sure that her mother had loved her.

Mistletoe wasn't exactly a hotspot of crime, and it's odd, since these weren't his children, but he couldn't stop the protective instinct that compelled him to say to Warren, "Stand here beside your sister and don't let anything happen to her," as he set her car seat on the floor in the bathroom.

He shifted Trevor on his hip and grabbed Garrett's hand, leading him over to a stall, since the urinals were too tall for his short legs.

He hadn't exactly gotten completely adept at working with one hand, but he was able to get Garrett on the toilet and was gratified to see that his underwear still looked dry.

Minnie had said something about pull-ups and that Garrett had been completely potty trained, but the recent upheavals in his life had caused him to regress.

Pull-ups were supposedly some kind of disposable underwear type things the kid could wear, but West hadn't had time to look into anything like that. He'd been working on getting his equipment ready for planting, and as warm as it had been, he should already have seed in the ground.

He didn't have time to go shopping for disposable underwear. It looked like it didn't matter, and he would have to make time.

He did the best he could at getting everybody's hands washed, including his, and managed to herd everyone out of the bathroom.

The lunch rush seemed to be in full swing, and there were no seats.

Just his luck.

"Hang on a second, boys." He stood in front of the bathroom doors, scanning the restaurant, looking to see if anybody was getting ready to leave.

He couldn't see a single table that looked like they were finished.

Man, he shouldn't have tried to get up and get some work done out in the barn before he had to go to the appointment.

Minnie had been too weak this morning to cook anything, and he should have been in helping her.

He just hadn't been prepared to have a family of five dropped on his lap ten days ago. And he'd been even less prepared to start taking care of them all by himself.

To learn how to handle children, to cook for more than himself, and to do this whole diaper/baby/bottle/little people who can't do anything for themselves thing.

One at a time. That's the way it should have been.

"Where we going to sit, Mr. West?" Leave it to Warren to ask the obvious question.

The one he didn't have an answer to.

"If you don't mind going in the back, you guys can all sit down back there, and I'll take care of you there." Poppy had come over, with her smile and her pep and her eternal optimism that right now West just wanted to smash into the ground with the heel of his boot. Either before or after he grabbed a hold of it with both hands and buried his whole face in it.

She tore him in directions he didn't want to go.

"That's okay. I was going to take the kids to the park anyway. I guess that's what we'll do and come back later."

"But I'm hungry," Garrett said with a whine in his voice.

Of all the children, Garrett seemed to be taking the changes the worst.

"Of course you are. I think kids your age are always hungry," Poppy said with a smile, scrunching down a little so he could see her better.

Garrett shrank back and tucked himself behind Warren with only his head sticking out as he looked with wide eyes at the lady who was smiling at him.

"I am not."

West bit his tongue over the automatic correction that came to his lips. If it were his kid, he'd be talking to him about contradicting an adult. But it wasn't his kid, and Garrett had been through a lot. He wasn't getting a pass for the rest of his life, but he could get a pass for a little while as his mom fought cancer.

He hoped Poppy could see the apology on his face, but she didn't look at him.

"But you are now," she said, sweetly and softly and with a smile that, if she turned it on West, he would never be able to resist.

Apparently, Garrett and he had some things in common, even if he didn't have the disposable underwear issues that Garrett did.

At least not yet. He almost felt like he could be driven to it at this point.

"I'm hungry. I want French fries." Garrett stepped out a little from behind West's leg and took a tentative step toward Poppy.

She didn't move toward him, almost as though she knew his bravery was tenuous and didn't want to make a move that would push him back.

From the little bit he'd been around her in church and now with these kids, it seemed that Poppy had been around a good many children.

He assumed she was as innocent as the baby in the carrier but had grown up in church, maybe working in the nurseries, and knew about children from that.

Somehow, he wondered about the accuracy of that assumption.

"I can get you some French fries. Would you like a hot dog to go along with that?" she asked, still not crowding on Garrett's space, allowing him to make the moves.

He nodded his head yes. "And I want chocolate milk."

"Done."

She straightened, and those hazel eyes that seemed to be green at times, and then brown, and then both, met West's, and he forgot to breathe.

Forgot about the kids in his arms.

Forgot about the empty blackness in his soul.

Her smile did that to him.

Her laugh was deadly.

He needed to stay away from her. She was everything he ever wanted and all the things he couldn't have.

He squared his jaw and made sure his face was stoic.

"Good morning, Grumpy. Did you miss the sunshine this morning? How can you be so angry looking on such a beautiful day?"

"If you would have had my day, you'd know," he growled. "Plus, Peppy. It's afternoon."

Of course, her smile didn't dim. If anything, it got brighter.

"My day's been going great, thanks for asking." Her green eyes got bigger if that were possible. "Now, are you going to take these poor starving children to the back and sit down with them or not?"

"Or not."

"Okay. You need me to kick someone out? Which table?" She turned and leaned toward him like they were sharing a secret.

It was all he could do to not move back. Poppy was definitely not the person he wanted to share secrets with.

"How about Mr. and Mrs. Ritchie? They're in their 90s if they're a day. They shouldn't be having a whole table to themselves."

"It will take them thirty minutes just to get up from the table and walk away. Plus, they're nice."

"They *are* nice. But I'm sure they'd give up their table for you." She crossed her arm over her stomach and tapped her pointy little chin. West had never really noticed it before, but her face was kind of in the shape of a heart. Fitting, with her personality.

Not that he cared.

"I guess we could get Blakely and Martin to get up. I've just delivered their drinks, and they're still waiting on their food, but they meet here every week, they've been best friends forever, and I suppose they'd be willing to give their table up for you and your four children. She's your sister, after all."

Blakely had been so engrossed in talking and laughing with Martin that she hadn't even seen that he'd walked in. "First of all, they're not my kids. Second of all, I'm not putting anyone out of their table." She'd been joking, but laughing with her was dangerous, and he wouldn't do it. "I'm taking the kids to the park."

"That's fine. Tell me what you all want, and I'll bring the food when I get off my shift in thirty minutes."

"You don't have to do that."

"I don't recall saying I did. I offered. Actually, I didn't even offer. I just said I'd do it."

"I can feed the kids."

"No one said you couldn't." She put her hands on her hips. "I wanted to do something nice. I know that's really hard for you to understand."

"I understand nice. I just don't understand ridiculously happy all the time over everything. That doesn't make any sense. *You* don't make sense."

"I would say someone needs to go back home and get out of the other side of the bed, but I'm pretty sure both sides are equally bad at your house. Maybe you need a whole new bed."

"I gave my bed to Minnie."

Immediately, her face dropped, although the glow of serene happiness never diminished. He felt bad immediately for being the reason that there was even a shadow of anything other than extreme joy on her face. He'd feel terrible if the happiness that he complained about so incessantly actually disappeared.

"I'm sorry." He hadn't meant to say that; the words just slipped out. Poppy wasn't meant to look anything but happy. She wasn't meant to have anything but joy and happiness in her life.

"No. It's me that's sorry. You do have a lot going on, and I've just been picking on you like we always do. I'll try to be more considerate."

Of course, she took the blame. Which made him feel like more of a heel than he already did. Why did she push all his buttons and get his defenses up?

It was like he couldn't be too nice to her, or she'd see what was really in his heart.

Even he didn't know what was really in his heart.

"It's me. Just a lot of stuff going on at my house. I'm used to being alone." That was absolutely true.

Poppy nodded, her eyes sweeping the children and her heart on her sleeve. It was obvious she couldn't see anything in distress without wanting to spread her positive energy or whatever it was around.

Part of him wanted to roll his eyes, and part of him wanted to wrap his arms around her and protect her from all the hurt the world could throw at her.

Didn't she know when she let herself be so open that all she was asking for was a great big pile of heartache? Hadn't she lived long enough to see that?

"Do you know what the kids want? I'll put an order in?" she asked. Then her smile descended on Warren, who blinked from its brightness. "I bet you can tell me what you want. You're big enough to know."

"I want French fries. And I want chocolate milk too. But I hate hot dogs."

"I can put extra onions on yours if you want."

West almost laughed. What kid liked onions?

"Barf me out the door," Warren said, sticking a finger in his mouth and his tongue out.

"Then you can give your onions to West, because he loves them."

"If it has onions on it, I'm not touching it." Warren crossed his arms over his chest and put his nose in the air.

The corners of Poppy's mouth crinkled. It was obvious from look on her face that she thought he was the most adorable kid ever.

"I don't like onions either," West said, more to prove her wrong, but he really didn't like onions. "I think you could be safe to leave onions out of the whole order."

Gabriella started to fuss, and he bounced her car seat, hoping she could hold it together until they got to the park at least. He had bottles in the baby bag, but he hadn't been able to sling that pink thing over his shoulder and still feel like a man, so he left it in his truck.

"Well, then maybe we can trade. I'll give you my hamburger, and you can give me your onions, and we'll both be happy."

"I'm starting to think I know why you're not married."

"Because I choose not to be," she said over her shoulder with a lowered head, still writing on her notepad.

"I thought that was an apple you were eating the other day, but I bet it was one of those purple onions."

"Might have been. Don't they keep vampires away or something?" She pursed her lips. "Funny you're still around."

"That's garlic." But he couldn't bring himself to retaliate about the vampire comment. It hit too close to home. Too close to the darkness and the negative blackness that always seemed to seep into his soul.

If she noticed, she didn't say anything.

"What do you want?" she asked, straightening from her bent-over position in front of the boys.

"Burger and fries is fine. Bring one for yourself. I'll pay for it." He turned just a little, jiggling the car seat as Gabriella started fussing more earnestly. "You can grab my wallet from my back pocket."

Her eyes opened wide, almost like he'd suggested she skin the baby and hang it over a spit.

Even after Race and Penny had adopted him and his siblings, his life hadn't exactly been on the straight and narrow. He supposed his past defined him more than he wanted to admit.

"I'm sorry. I'd deck the guy who said that to my sister."

"No, it's me. I guess I'm a prude. Normal people are fine with that." There it was again, the little dim in her smile, the little dip in the peppy words she used. The cause was all him.

He didn't even know why he noticed. It wasn't like he spent his life going around wondering whether some woman was smiling as bright as she had been or not.

Only with Poppy.

"Warren, grab my wallet out of my pocket, please."

Warren thought it was pretty cool to be able to grab his wallet, and his grin was big and wide as he pulled the leather pouch out.

"Here you go." He pointed it at West, like West didn't already have both hands full or he would have gotten the wallet himself.

"I'll take it." Poppy reached her hand out and took the wallet carefully from Warren.

Opening it, she said, "Is there a card?"

"There should be enough cash in there to cover it. Or you can use my card if you want. Your choice."

When she opened it, the picture that he always kept in there stared out at her, and she paused. It was the last one that had been taken of his birth parents and his siblings. Her breath hitched.

It was only a second or two as her eyes swept the picture, and maybe it was fanciful thinking on his part, but it was like she picked him out of the group of children.

"Your birth parents?" she asked softly, the glow still there but more of a warm, muted feeling than the bright sunshine that she usually exuded.

"Yeah." Had he wanted her to see it? It wasn't a picture he went around showing anyone. Of course, he didn't usually go around giving his wallet to just anyone either. Ever, actually.

Poppy was different. She was different in a lot of different ways.

"You guys look happy." Her finger hovered above the picture, almost, but not quite, touching.

Her words were soft, all the vivacity erased.

There was compassion in her eyes, not pity, thankfully, when she looked up at him.

Why did he have the feeling that she knew how he felt? It was almost like there was a camaraderie in her gaze that said she'd been there.

But she hadn't.

That must be how she related to people so well. She could make them feel like she knew how they felt.

She pulled her phone out of her apron pocket. "I need to get back to work. Give me your phone number, and I'll text you if I need you."

She hadn't asked for his number. Just demanded. But because it was Poppy, and he knew she wasn't using some underhanded technique to try to get his number, which had happened to him more times than he could count, he rattled it off without thinking.

"I'll find you in the park." She glanced at the clock on the wall. "In twenty-five minutes."

He nodded. Still a little in disbelief that he was walking away from his wallet, and that he'd just given her his number, and trying to remember that he didn't even like her.

Chapter Five

Poppy juggled the Styrofoam take-out containers as she gently eased the bag up around them.

"Thanks so much for letting me go early," she said to Kelly who was tying an apron around her waist. It wasn't anything for Kelly to pitch in anywhere the diner needed help. That's what an owner did, after all.

"If anyone needed help, it was West. I'm glad someone's giving him a hand. I'm not sure what's going to go on with that lady...what was her name?"

"Minnie."

"Yeah. Minnie. What a sad situation."

Poppy couldn't disagree. She felt bad for West, too. He'd definitely looked overwhelmed with all the kids.

Of all the men in Mistletoe, West was probably the least likely to have children. He definitely didn't seem like a kid kinda guy. He didn't seem like a marrying kind of guy. He seemed like a let me go to my farm and leave me alone kinda guy.

She supposed that's why girls seemed to buzz around him. They liked the challenge. Well, she didn't need that kind of challenge. She had absolutely no intention of getting married and even less of having children. She loved them, of course she did, and her heart was pulled toward any child in her vicinity, but after what she'd already gone through, there was no way.

Shouldn't that be up to the Lord?

She didn't need to have that voice in her head, and she shoved it, rudely, aside.

God and she were in total and complete agreement on this. She knew it. He would never ask her to go through that type of thing again. And the best way to make sure that it didn't happen was to not have a family of her own.

"It's so pretty out. It's hard to believe that they're calling for that huge storm later in the week." Kelly glanced at the window as she arranged the plates on her serving tray. "They said it might even snow. Of course, they say that every winter, and then we get like a dusting. If that. And all the kids are thinking that they might go home from school early, and we barely get any flakes. It's always a bust. I believe the rain though. Looks like a lot."

"If we get what they're calling for, there's definitely going to be some flooding in the low areas."

"We can use that precipitation though, after last summer which was really dry." Kelly put mustard and ketchup on her tray and grabbed a bunch of straws, sticking them in the pocket of her apron. "Enjoy your lunch date," she called as Poppy grabbed a large bag in each hand and started for the door.

"It's not a lunch date," she said with a little laugh but also very seriously over her shoulder.

Kelly just pursed her lips and lifted a shoulder, wiggling her fingers before lifting the tray of food and walking to table twelve.

Was that what everyone was going to think?

If she took this food to the park and ate with West, were people going to have them married by next year this time? Were they going to be an item, even if they weren't?

Poppy didn't want that. In fact, that was one of the last things she wanted. She definitely didn't want him to think that she wanted to be linked with him; she didn't want to be linked with anyone.

Still, she couldn't control what other people thought, so she might as well not worry about it. She'd already told him she was bringing him food, and her lunch was in here too, so she was going to spend an hour at the park with West. If the town of Mistletoe had a heyday with that, that was their problem.

Maybe she should say something to West about it. Make sure that he was under no illusions as to what she thought. The direct route always seemed to be the best way.

Jerking her head down in a firm nod to herself, happy she'd gotten things figured out, she marched down the sidewalk.

It didn't take long for her stride to slow though. For being early February, the day was gorgeous.

Maybe people weren't expecting it, or maybe most folk with young children had those kids taking naps after lunch, but West and Minnie's children were the only ones at the park.

Not that it was much of a park. Mistletoe wasn't that big. But there were some slides and swings and other playground equipment and a small reflecting pond where children ten and under were allowed to fish.

From the way Warren was standing at the pond peering into it, Poppy assumed he probably wished he had a pole.

West had Gabriella in one arm, snuggled down into a blanket with hat on, and a bottle in her mouth while he pushed Trevor on the baby swing and Garrett on the regular swing.

Poppy had to admire the way the guy multitasked. She wasn't even sure she could do all that, and she'd had a lot of experience in nurseries.

As busy as he was with the kids, his head went up as she walked in the gate to the play area. She held up the bags and then motioned to the nearest picnic table.

He nodded, and if she wasn't mistaken, one side of his mouth picked up. The man must be hungry. That was almost a smile.

He said Warren's name as he slowed the swings.

She wasn't quite sure how he had gotten Trevor into the swing with the baby in his arm, so Poppy set the food on the table and jogged over to give him a hand getting him out.

"Definitely happy to see the food. And I can't say I don't appreciate your help too," he said, like he too wasn't sure how he was going to get Trevor out.

"Have to say, I'm impressed. I'm not sure I could do what all you're doing."

"Sure you could. It just takes practice." He said it sarcastically, because they both knew he'd had all those kids for less than two weeks.

"You had an awful lot dumped on your lap."

"And I rose to the occasion."

"Humbly, of course," she said with a lifted brow and not a little sarcasm of her own.

"Some people are just naturally good."

"When you meet one of those, would ya introduce me to them?" she asked, lifting Trevor and pressing her cheek against his chubby red one.

His little hands flailed, and his legs kicked. "No! No! No!"

"I think that means he wants to keep swinging," she said, not really to West, because they weren't really having a conversation.

"He was having a good time."

"Aren't you hungry, buddy?" she asked between yells in the voice she used for children, which was not exactly baby talk but not loaded with the sarcasm that she had been using on West either. He brought out the worst in her. Which was another reason for her to steer clear of him. Somewhere, in some sermon or self-help book, it was written very clearly that one should stay away from negative influences in one's life.

West was definitely a negative influence. No one could make her want to spit nails faster than him. And usually with just a look. He didn't even need words.

"No! No!"

"You really need to teach your child how to say yes," she said, pressing Trevor's body against hers and making sure the swing didn't hit him when his foot caught.

"I'll get right on that. Right after I figure out how to juggle cooking and cleaning and changing pooped underwear." He said the last a little lower, although Garrett had jumped off the swing and run over to the picnic table with Warren.

"Still?"

"Yeah. Minnie said he was trained, but all of this upheaval has caused him to regress. I've gone through four pairs so far this morning."

"You should use pull-ups. They're like disposable underwear. Isn't that what he's wearing?"

"I've never even heard of pull-ups until a couple days ago. In fact, if you had said pull-up to me, I would have thought horizontal bar and elbow grease."

She laughed. "And rightfully so. Maybe I can stop by the store later on today and grab you some. I'm guessing shopping with these guys is a bit of a challenge as well."

"I haven't tried that yet. I did go to the grocery store twice, but Minnie stayed with them both times. Although Warren seems to want to go everywhere I go, and he came with me."

"I suppose it's gossip if I ask about the father?" Trevor had calmed down and relaxed against her.

They started walking toward the table.

"Probably, although I'm curious too. I haven't asked Minnie. There haven't been that many times where she's been awake but not consumed with spending time with the kids. I can't believe how much work these little guys are."

West held the car seat in his free hand and somehow managed to keep the baby in the blanket and the bottle all upright and working with his other.

"You must have been good at sports when you were in school."

"Never played them."

He didn't elaborate, and Poppy didn't feel like his statement left any room for her questions. Of which she had a few.

But she shouldn't, because she kept telling herself she wasn't interested.

They worked on getting the kids situated again, with her getting the Styrofoam containers out of the bag and West settling Garrett and Warren down at the table and helping them open their containers.

Poppy slipped in opposite West with Trevor on her lap. And she helped him bow his head and fold his hands while West prayed.

The act itself surprised her, although she supposed she was being judgmental to allow it to.

After the kids had settled down eating and she was spooning applesauce into Trevor, she said, "This is getting to be a habit. You and me feeding these children."

West had just taken a big bite of his hamburger, which he set back down on his Styrofoam container, and chewed while he gently patted Gabriella's back and bounced her carefully. It was a little bit before he chewed and swallowed.

"So you're worried people are going to talk about us?"

She hadn't expected him to pick up on that. "I guess I kind of thought you would give me a sarcastic answer, and I would have to explain it to you."

"I live here too. I've been here longer than you. I definitely know how things work."

"I just wanted to make sure you understood. I'm not trying to get people to talk about us, and I am not trying to get anywhere with you. Just saw a need."

For once he seemed serious, not sarcastic, and he nodded, his face not showing any emotion but not glowering either, which is what it always seemed to when she was around.

"Not just seeing it. Not just saying it. I appreciate you doing something about it. I feel like I'm drowning here sometimes." His eyes narrowed and his lips pressed together like he hadn't meant to say even that much.

But then, like he needed to say more, he continued, "I don't know what Minnie's plans are, and I can't even bring myself to ask. She's got so much going on and so much heartache and hardship..." He shook his head. "I don't know why she even came to me. I'm the last person in the world who would know what to do with kids."

His eyes skimmed over to Warren and Garrett who were sitting across the table from each other talking about the fish that Warren had seen in the pond and were not paying them the slightest bit of attention.

"But I can't say anything. I can't tell her I can't do it. I can't tell her to go somewhere else. I can't even tell her that I want to bring someone in to help me. I just... I guess she'll know more after her appointment today, but she already has so much going on I just can't not be strong for her."

He looked down, his hand never stopping its rhythmic tapping on the baby's back as he seemed to be warring inside himself. What he wanted versus what he knew he needed to do.

This was a totally new side of West. Poppy worked to keep her jaw from dropping down on the picnic table. He seemed almost... human.

Somehow, this didn't seem like the time for their usual sarcastic banter, though.

"It probably doesn't help anything, but I've been sitting here admiring how natural you look with Gabriella. Feeding the baby a bottle and pushing two little kids on the swings while watching that Warren didn't fall into the pond was far more than what I feel like I'm capable of doing. I can't tell you feel like you're overwhelmed. You look like you have everything under control."

"Yeah. It's just an illusion. Isn't that life?"

Traces of bitterness ran through his words. That bitterness surprised her too. It also gave her the feeling that there was a lot more to his words than what she saw on the surface. A lot more to West than what anyone guessed.

Including her.

"No. It's possible to live a real life. Real. Not pretending to be something you're not. But you really are that thing you want to be."

"That sounds like Pollyanna talking. Peppy Pollyanna."

Gabriella let out a soft burp along with some white liquid with just a few chunks which landed on and ran down West's shirt.

"Crap. Forgot the burp rag."

"Crap," Warren said, from the end of the picnic table.

"Crap, crap, crap," Garrett echoed.

West's jaw flexed, and his eyes closed. Like he was digging deep, for patience or for wisdom, Poppy wasn't sure.

"I don't think that's a word your mother probably wants you to say." She looked at Warren first. He looked down at the table. Of course, he knew precisely that his mother didn't want him to say that word.

"And Garrett," she said sweetly and softly, because she was a stranger, and they weren't her kids, but if she were dying of cancer, and someone else were raising her children, she would really appreciate it if they would teach them to do right and not just let them get away with anything even though they were going through a hard time.

Of course, she wanted people to have compassion for her children. But she didn't want her children spoiled, either.

Garrett, a French fry sticking out of his mouth, looked up at her with big brown eyes.

"Don't say that word. There's lots of other words you can say instead." She squinted her eyes and pretended to think really hard. "Like...French fries!" she said, like she just pulled that word way out of the blue and hadn't thought of it because he had one hanging out of his mouth.

Garrett giggled. "French fries."

"Hey, give me that," Warren said as Garrett pulled a fry off his Styrofoam container.

She lowered her voice and looked at West. "There's something very satisfying about saying French fry. Probably better than that other word you had."

"That's another area where I've been struggling. Every single thing I do, they copy. There's nothing like a kid to magnify your faults."

That was so true.

"Nothing like a kid to show you where your faults are." Her lack of patience, her selfishness, her inability to want the best for someone else over herself. "I've been told it gets easier."

"I'm hoping that they don't stay young long enough for it to get to be easy." He sighed. "That sounded terrible. I'm sorry."

"No. I understand. This isn't what you'd been planning for your life. I guess sometimes we just have these bumps in the road." Boy, did she ever know about bumps in the road.

West's head lowered, and he spoke low. "Don't look, but there's a lady from church. She's been staring at us for at least ten minutes." He jerked his head over toward the sidewalk where the gate to the playground was. "I guess that'll be another bump in the road when we walk into church on Sunday morning and everyone expects us to be sitting together."

"We'll just not live up to expectations at that point." She certainly wasn't going to sit with anyone just because people expected her to. And she was one hundred percent sure that West wouldn't either.

"I just hope they don't give my parents any ideas. Sometimes, my folks get crazy thoughts in their head, and somehow, they manage to finagle things into happening."

"Really?"

"Sure. It happened with my brothers. I'm pretty sure Denver wouldn't have ended up with Natalie if it hadn't been for my dad's meddling."

"But they're so happy together! I mean, Natalie is perfect for him. And he's amazing with her. Just looking at them makes you believe in love."

He snorted. But then he sighed again. "Yeah. You're right. But none of their hocus-pocus can work with me. And I'm warning you, only because you're helping me today, that you better stay away so they don't start trying to work it on you if you don't want to end up married to some poor sot." He shivered, only partially joking, she thought. "I pity the poor girl they sic on me. I'm not going down without a fight."

He seemed to be lifting a little bit of the darkness that had been surrounding him, and that last was said with more than a little humor.

"I'll be fighting right alongside you then, because I'm not interested in any hocus-pocus in my life either. I'm definitely not going through that again."

"Going through what?"

She shook her head. West had maybe said more to her than he intended to. But she wasn't doing the same. There was no way she was talking about her past. Not with West. He'd make fun of her for it. One of his favorite pastimes was to call her Pollyanna. Like being Pollyanna was a bad thing. He had no idea how awful it was to be the opposite of a Pollyanna.

"I think that looks like your mother and Minnie," she said as a car pulled in behind West's pickup between the diner and the playground along the street.

"I believe you're right. Just in time," West said as he looked over at the boys who were finishing up their meals.

Chapter Six

*M*innie stayed in the car, but Miss Penny walked over to them, and they were just putting the Styrofoam containers back in the bags when she arrived at the picnic table.

"How's everything going today?" she asked with the typical upbeat tone that defined her personality.

Come to think of it, Poppy was a lot like his mother. Funny that Poppy annoyed him so.

Although she hadn't annoyed him today.

Actually, when she brought supper, she hadn't then, either.

Maybe it was him.

Poppy glanced at him as though waiting for him to answer, but his mother was looking at her, so he grabbed one of the napkins that Poppy had set under the can of formula and started swiping his shoulder. All the throw up had pretty much already sunk in, and in his experience, he would be smelling it the rest of the day. Or at least until he changed.

Actually, he was kind of getting used to it. Gabriella was almost cute enough to make it worthwhile. Almost.

"It's a beautiful day. And I think the kids are enjoying finally going out and playing and getting to eat outside." Poppy looked around at the boys when she said that and jiggled Trevor in one arm while she grabbed a napkin to give to Warren to wipe his face and another one to wipe Garrett's for him. "I think the question is how did things go with you?"

Penny's face fell, not a lot, but enough they knew the news wasn't good.

Penny's eyes went to the boys, who were arguing about who ate the most French fries, before she looked between Poppy and West. "After explaining the tests she'd had done last week, the doctor recommended hospice. She has waited too long. And there's nothing they can do."

West's chest felt like it seized before his heart started thumping his chest. Angry thoughts slammed like a sledgehammer on a wall, tearing down and destroying.

Even though he'd suspected as much, he didn't want to admit it, didn't want to face it. Didn't want the children to not have a mother. Didn't want to have to deal with everything that had been thrust on him.

When Penny had taken her in for the tests last week, he prayed more fervently than he had in years that everything would be okay.

He supposed it shouldn't surprise him that God ignored that prayer, like he'd ignored so many others.

Or maybe he hadn't ignored it. Just answered with a big resounding "no." A no that felt mean, and unkind, and unfathomable, and most definitely not fair or right.

I thought you were a God of justice. Where's the justice in this?

He felt selfish even thinking about himself, but he didn't want to be saddled with four kids. He hadn't asked for that. Of course, it shouldn't be his first concern, but why had Minnie chosen him?

His heart bled for the children too. He spent almost two weeks with them, which felt like a lifetime in some ways and felt like he was in the twilight zone in others.

Gabriella stretched and snuggled down further into his arm.

Maybe part of his resentment was the fact that he was afraid he was falling in love with Minnie's children.

What was he going to do? When they left, it would hurt worse than anything he'd felt since his parents died.

He hadn't wanted to lose his heart again.

Hadn't wanted to give anything the opportunity to break it like it had been broken before.

He'd been determined to keep himself apart, to not let anything in. And yet, these children, as imperfect as they were, as much work as they were, they were sweet souls who needed someone to take care of them, love them, and even more so now, now that he knew their mother wasn't going to be in the picture much longer.

His mother's concerned face seemed to search his, but he didn't meet her eyes. He loved her, appreciated the sacrifice that she and Race had made in order to take him and his siblings in when no one else would. Six kids was a lot for anyone; six kids who were almost all teenagers was more than they could expect anyone to do.

Race and Penny had jumped in and had done just as good a job as anyone could expect birth parents to do. Had loved them like their own, had disciplined them like their own, and hadn't given them any slack while they hadn't withheld any love either.

He'd been blessed to have two of the most amazing sets of parents in the entire world.

He looked at the kids at the table and the baby in his arms, innocent and trusting. They weren't going to have what he had.

How could he even think about himself when faced with that reality?

Even though that question was totally reasonable and rational, he still resented the fact that his life had been upended. And he'd been forced to come face-to-face with the thing that he most feared.

Losing someone he loved again.

"I imagine Minnie's probably tired. We'll get this stuff gathered up and get her home so she can take a rest." She'd barely been out of bed in the time she'd spent at his house. She had to be exhausted.

"Maybe Poppy can take the kids over to the truck. I'd like to talk to you."

He jerked his head in assent, then dug his keys out of his pocket after putting Gabriella in her car seat and buckling her. He handed her off, and Poppy took her without saying anything, Trevor on one hip and the car seat carried in the other hand, his keys in her teeth.

He didn't even mention the unsanitariness of that. No point. After having the kids for as long as he had, he understood a person did what they had to do.

Penny waited until they got to the gate before she came around the picnic table and sat down, her hand landing on his knee.

He put his hand, bigger and browner, over top of it. "You're going to give me the lowdown?"

Penny took a deep breath in and blew it out, watching as Minnie carefully got out of her car when Poppy approached it. The boys ran to her, and Poppy put a hand out as though trying to slow them down. Minnie looked like a stiff wind would blow her away.

"Hospice means hospice. I don't think I need to spell that out for you."

"No."

"I don't know if she's talked to you about the pain she's been in, but that's going to be an issue."

"No. She hasn't said a word."

"I figured not. There's probably a lot of things she hasn't said."

"Are you going to?"

Penny shook her head, but it wasn't a no; it was almost an *I don't know where to start.* "She found out about the cancer about the same time she found out about Gabriella. She had to make a choice. Obviously, you can see what her choice was. Since they knew about the cancer, they induced her early and hoped they might be able to get a jump on treatment. There were some delays, some issues regarding her insurance, and of course having cancer and a newborn and three other children was overwhelming. That's how she ended up with you."

West looked away. He could hardly imagine a sacrifice like that.

"Where's the dad?"

"He was working for a pig farm in Iowa, and he fell into the manure pit. They didn't find the body until they drained the pit."

West lived in a farming community, and agricultural accidents were not uncommon to hear about. Still, he cringed. He couldn't imagine.

"I don't think the first two are his. And I don't think they were married. She didn't exactly live a straight-line life. But there's no doubt she wants the best for her children."

"Sounds like you two had quite the talk."

"She's scared. Not really of dying." Penny rubbed her free hand along her leg, seeming to be trying to figure out how to say what needed to be said. "She's scared for her children. She knows she hasn't done the best or made the best choices for them, but she really wanted to correct that, and she thought she was heading in the right direction. Then this past year, things unraveled, and right now, her sole focus is doing right by her kids."

"So we're looking for a foster family?"

Penny didn't say anything for a while, letting the silence wash over them.

A soft breeze, flowing over the damp earth fresh from winter, clean and new, stirred between them.

This was with his favorite time of year. The anticipation and promise of new life.

Seeds in the ground, plants coming up, everything wide open. All the mistakes and bad luck of the past year forgotten. All the possibilities of the growing season ahead, ripe with opportunities and the thought that anything could happen with just a little hard work, having the chips fall in his favor, and the year could be better than anything he'd ever dreamed.

He wasn't afraid of hard work, and he felt that luck followed that. He wasn't afraid to dream big either.

Except this year wasn't shaping up to be like anything he'd planned. Certainly not like his dreams.

"I think she'd like them to be with her during her last days," his mom said slowly, pinching her pant leg together before brushing it out and looking up at him. "I think she's hoping that she can stay with you...until the end."

He never intended to meet his mother's gaze, wanted to look anywhere but, but somehow as his eyes skimmed across hers, they caught and held.

Her expression held compassion, and her hand squeezed his while the breeze ruffled her hair and she pushed it back. "I understand that's not what you want. I'm sure I can make arrangements for someone else to help. We could find a bunch of different places to take all the children." Her eyebrows shifted just a little of that, and he figured she was probably thinking about him and his siblings and how they'd been farmed out when his parents died.

"I'll keep them."

How could he say anything else? How could he not do for these kids what Race and Penny had done for him? "Until after she passes."

Penny nodded. "It's inevitable."

"How long?"

"The doctor didn't know. Could be days. She could last months. He'd said less than six."

West nodded. Not surprised.

"His biggest concern was managing the pain. We've gotten some prescriptions, and hospice will help."

West's jaw twitched. Hopefully what the doctor had done would work. The kids didn't need to see their mother suffering as well as dying.

"There were two things she'd said to me that she wanted more than anything."

Finally, something he might be able to take action on. "Yeah?"

"This was in the waiting room. Before she heard the diagnosis. I think she thought she had more time."

Didn't they all? Didn't everyone think they had more time? Because they thought they had forever, they took the people they loved for granted? Thinking there would always be another day, another weekend, another vacation. No one ever thought it was going to be the last.

As a teenager, that was certainly the way he'd thought.

Even though he'd experienced the shortness of life and the abruptness of its ending, he still made the same mistake.

"I think that's a mistake we all make." It was him being honest.

Penny nodded. There was no way she couldn't agree with that. "She talked about how Gabriella had been born the day after Christmas. And how she'd wanted Gabriella to have a Christmas with her. Just one. For the pictures and all that. I know that's not going to happen now. Not without a miracle."

His mother didn't have to ask him to pray. Before she'd even stopped, even though he knew it would make for a long year for him, he'd asked the Lord to give Minnie a Christmas with her kids.

"That would give her four months more than the six the doctor thought she could have."

"I'm pretty sure the doctor was being very optimistic when he said six months. I would say it's more a matter of weeks," Penny said slowly.

"I appreciate you guys sending meals out. That's been helpful." Maybe it was a bit of a subject change, but he didn't want to talk about death any more than the next guy. Didn't want to think about it. Didn't want to face it. And now it was going to be in his house.

"Poppy has organized all of that. If you want to thank someone, you can thank her." His mother turned her hand over, patting his knuckles. "She's a good girl."

"I know she is. Too good for me." He didn't mean for that last bit to slip out, but since it had... "I don't want people talking about us.

There's nothing there. There never will be. Maybe you can make sure people know that."

His mother bit her lips, and that couldn't be a smile at the corners of her mouth. Couldn't be. They were talking about four children who were soon to be orphans and a mother who was dying. She wouldn't be smiling. Not now. And especially not over Poppy and him.

"Be serious, Mom. The very last person in the world I want to be stuck with for any amount of time would be someone who's perpetually smiling and in such an annoyingly good mood that you can hardly hear yourself think."

"Her good mood makes it impossible for you to think?" his mother asked, with more than a little disbelief in her voice. "Don't you mean her good mood makes it impossible for you to continue in your bad mood?"

She always had a way of cutting right to the issue. Now that he was an adult, he appreciated it more than he had as teen.

"I always gave you more trouble than any of my siblings. Thanks for putting up with me."

Penny's eyes widened. As well they should, probably. He wasn't sure he'd ever said anything to his parents about that before.

Maybe it was because of Minnie, the thoughts of dying, and the thoughts of how he took the people closest to him for granted.

He supposed it was a good thing he didn't have a wife, because he'd probably treat her the same way. He'd get used to having someone around, and there would be nothing special anymore. She'd just be there.

Until she wasn't.

Chapter Seven

Poppy slipped the apron over her head and reached for the strings, tying them in the back in an action that felt automatic as she'd done it so many times.

It was hard to get West and those kids out of her head. She'd talked to Penny later, who had told her that Minnie wasn't expected to make it more than a few months at most.

The kids had already been through so much. Poor Warren and Garrett, and Trevor was such a sweet little thing.

Then of course there was Gabriella, a baby who would never know her mother or father.

Beyond that, West had looked amazingly handsome holding her. Even now, just thinking about it pulled her heartstrings. How could a man who was being so tender and gentle look so strong at the same time?

"Do you have a second before your shift starts?"

Miss Penny's voice startled her out of her thoughts, and she whirled around, her hand on her heart.

"Oh my. I wasn't paying the slightest bit of attention, and you scared me." She laughed a little, sounding nervous but finding herself funny. How could she be so deeply in thought about a man she didn't even like and kids she barely even knew?

Her smile faded at Penny's serious look.

"Do you remember when you first came here a couple of years ago, you told me that you had given the church's number to the institute where your mother was staying?"

Immediately, Poppy's chest froze, and the hand that had dropped from her heart shot back like she could grab her heart and keep it from jumping out.

"Yes?" She couldn't keep the trepidation out of her voice.

"There was a call last night from them."

It could have been about Hazel, her little sister, but it almost had to be about her mother. She'd been doing well, holding down a job and taking care of Hazel. Poppy went back to Missouri, of course, to visit, for holidays mostly. Although she hadn't made it for Christmas this year. She thought her mother was doing well. The last time she'd been there, she even thought there might be a hint of romance.

"She's back on a suicide watch. The call was about Hazel."

Poppy closed her eyes and clenched her fists. She couldn't look at her little sister without seeing the sisters she'd lost. Hazel looked just like Rachel and Abigail with her fair curly hair and bright blue eyes.

Her brain was working slow, but thankfully, it was working.

"They need me to take her?"

Penny nodded. "If you can. The lady I talked to was very sensitive and understanding about your position and about how all this affects you. You've gone through the same thing your mother has, just from a different perspective. She didn't want this development to ruin the life you've built for yourself since the accident."

Accident. That word could encompass so many different scenarios. So many deaths.

"Hazel is not a complication. She's my sister. Can I go today and pick her up? After my shift?"

"That's the other thing I wanted to talk to you about." Penny put a hand on her arm, and somehow, Poppy found herself seated in a chair facing her, their knees almost touching.

"Pastor Race would like to put you on the church payroll."

"Really?" Poppy's brows had shot up. She already did a lot for the church, although it was all volunteer. She was fine with that. Honestly, she knew it probably wasn't healthy, but she had no goals or ambitions for her life beyond just surviving it. And helping other people. That's all she wanted.

The idea of working for the church was appealing but odd.

"That's strange. I already do everything I can, pretty much all of my spare time is spent working at the church. I don't need to be paid for it."

"Well, what he's thinking he wants you to do will require you quitting your job here."

Her eyes widened. "I love working here. I get to see everyone in town, talk to them." And there were no attachments. Not beyond a casual conversation, casual acquaintance. Of course, she cared about the people in her town. But it wasn't like a family.

"I know. We both do. And I don't want you to feel like you have to accept this offer. It's just one that Pastor and I feel is a really good fit for you. But again, no hard feelings, no pressure." Penny's gaze was intense, and her hand squeezed Poppy's, who suddenly felt cold and limp.

"What is this offer?" A new thought occurred to her. "And will I be able to do it with Hazel?"

Penny nodded. "It's actually perfect timing. Pastor and I had been talking about this before we got the call late last night."

An order came up, and the short order cook yelled at Kelly.

Penny waited for the bustle to die down. "We...we feel like with the way things are going with Minnie, someone from the church needs to be helping West with the children. For some reason, Minnie wants her kids with West. Even though I spent a lot of time talking to her, I still haven't figured out exactly why. Maybe West knows." Penny's shoulders went up, and her face seemed to say it didn't matter. "Regardless, West has a farm to run. And I know last year wasn't very good for crops with the lack of rainfall. This year looks like it's going to be excellent, at least there's no drought. But he needs to be able to get ready and get in the field."

Penny wasn't saying anything that Poppy didn't already know. So she just nodded along, waiting for whenever it would apply to her.

"We were hoping you would go and, if not stay with West, at least help him on a daily basis with the children. The church will pay for it, however long it lasts. And..." Here, she hesitated again, as though she didn't want to say what she was about to say. "Even after Minnie passes, we're going to need to figure something out with the children. Of course, they'll probably be sent to foster care, unless we can discuss this with Minnie and possibly find a solution here in Mistletoe."

That sounded sufficiently vague to not give any specifics of any solution that Penny might be thinking. But Poppy barely noticed.

They wanted her to go and practically live with West.

"I know West is our son, but he's also a member of our church. Our church takes care of the people in it. This has very little to do with the fact that West is ours and everything to do with the fact that West belongs to our church. Does that make sense?"

Penny tilted her head and gazed at Poppy. A direct gaze but one so filled with compassion and love that Poppy could hardly stand it.

It made her long for her mother and her family and everything she'd lost years ago.

Those were feelings she didn't want to feel. Part of the reason she was happy being a waitress at the diner and volunteering at the church was that she could distance herself from them and fight them with loads of happiness and joy.

There was nothing wrong with that.

But Hazel changed things.

Poppy couldn't keep working as a waitress and pay for child care for Hazel. Penny was offering her a way she could keep her sister and still make money. And maybe by the time she wasn't needed anymore—she couldn't say when Minnie died—her mother would be in such a position that she would be able to take Hazel back.

"And just in case you're wondering, this position would pay slightly more than your waitressing job because it would definitely entail more work." Penny named the figure that the church board had agreed on. It wasn't quite double what she was making as a waitress. "How about you take some time to pray about it and think about it. You can give me your answer—"

"I'll do it. When do you want me to start?" Poppy put a hand up. "Wait. I need to go pick up Hazel. I can't start until then."

"I've actually asked Blakely if she'll take over your shift today. She couldn't make it until one o'clock." Penny looked at her watch. "That's fifteen minutes. If you want, I'll check with Kelly and make sure it's okay, but you can probably go get Hazel now and be back tomorrow. You can start then."

Poppy tucked her hair behind her ear, thinking. "There were clothes that people had donated for the children that I was supposed to deliver out to the farm today."

Penny nodded. "If you don't mind, Paula has said she'll do that, and she's just waiting for a call from me."

Paula was painfully shy. Poppy tried to picture her standing up to West and couldn't. But Miss Penny wouldn't send her out if she didn't think Paula could handle it.

Come to think of it, opposites often attracted. Maybe Paula and West would hit it off.

Poppy tried to smile. "That's perfect. I don't need time to think about it. Everything seems to be falling into place, with Hazel coming and me being offered a job I can do and still have her with me, not to mention the family that needs help." No matter how painful it might be for her to help. No matter how much she might want to avoid West.

"Don't rush your trip." Penny reached into her purse and pulled out a slip of paper. "Before I forget, here's a number you can call to talk to someone about your mom and paperwork. Your mom has approved you taking Hazel, which will expedite things."

Poppy's fingers shook as she took the paper. Funny how she felt so in control of things when everything was going well, but as soon as there was one little wrinkle in the life that she'd built for herself, she felt weak and disoriented and like she was ready to crumble.

She straightened her back. She wasn't going to crumble.

The joy of the Lord is my strength.

That had become her life's verse.

"I'll be back by tomorrow night. I can start then."

There was that storm that everybody had been calling "the storm of the century," but she wasn't sure exactly what day it was supposed to hit. It didn't seem to be on Penny's radar, so she wasn't going to worry about it either.

"I meant it. Don't rush. The day after tomorrow will be soon enough. In the meantime, Paula can give West a hand if he needs it."

Chapter Eight

West dropped the pooped underwear into a plastic bag, tied the bag, shifted Trevor on his hip, and threw the bag into the bathroom trashcan.

That was the third pair today.

"I can't believe someone as little as you could have so much poop in his body," he said under his breath to Garrett who was splashing in the tub as the water ran freely into it.

At least his little butt wasn't brown anymore.

The doorbell rang, yet again. Was that the third or fourth time?

West wasn't sure, and he didn't really care. Surely Poppy would figure out that he was probably changing pooped underwear—what else did he do anymore—and would let herself in.

Tempted to yell that the door wasn't locked, he refrained.

"It's kind of expensive for me to be using one pair every time you poop. We either need to get diapers or those pull-up things."

Garrett totally ignored him, probably couldn't even hear him over the running water, and splashed happily.

"Maybe changing your underwear shouldn't be quite so much fun, then you wouldn't want to do it so often." Now there was an idea. What kid didn't want to get naked in the tub and splash around?

He almost laughed. Really, he didn't truly think that Garrett pooped his pants on purpose just to get in the tub, but hey, it seemed reasonable. Right now, he wouldn't mind that himself actually.

He had baby spit on both shoulders, and he was pretty sure that Trevor was leaking out of his diaper.

The only kid that hadn't put bodily fluids on him today yet was Warren, but the day was only half over. Yesterday, Warren had fallen and scraped his knee.

Blood counted.

There was plenty of time for more blood today.

He complained in his head, but he didn't really mean it. He supposed sarcasm was his natural defense against caring for these kids. Allowing his heart to be soft and tender toward their plight and commiserating with them would only lead to more pain.

It was so easy to relate to them. At least he'd been older when he lost his parents.

The doorbell rang again.

He shut the water off and grabbed a towel, having gotten good at using one arm to wrap it around Garrett's body and lift him out of the tub while not setting Trevor down, who seemed to have forgotten completely how to use his feet and cried every time they touched the floor.

"You'd think that confounded woman would figure out that I'm not coming to the door and just open it herself."

Poppy wasn't shy; surely she could let herself in. "Actually, I hate to even say this, but I'm really looking forward to seeing her smile today. I think we could all use it."

He held Garrett against his body and rubbed a little with the towel while looking in his eyes and nodding.

"Poppy?" Garrett said. "Sunday school."

West nodded. "Yep. Your Sunday school teacher. She's going to be here soon, with her smile and eternal optimism. Maybe she'll have a bag of pull-ups. Wouldn't that be nice?"

"I want truck pull-ups."

"Even if they have Barbie dolls on them, you're going to wear them."

"No. Dolls is for girls. Me want trucks."

He shouldn't have said that. Would it damage the kid if the pull-ups were pink and he made him wear them anyway? He supposed there was a school of thought that shouted an outraged no to that question.

Just because that school of thought was loud didn't make it right. Honestly, he wasn't really sure.

"If I wear Barbie doll pull-ups, will you wear them?"

Garrett's thunder brows eased, and the pouty look came off his face while his lips twitched. "No."

Figures. West got the impression from the look on Garrett's face that even though he wouldn't wear the Barbie doll pull-ups, he'd enjoy watching West wear them.

"I don't think I'm going to either. They might damage me."

Felt like he was already damaged. Barbie doll pull-ups probably weren't going to do anything to him that he hadn't already done to himself.

"We don't even know if she has pull-ups. Let's cross that bridge when we come to it, how about it?" He gave a decisive nod, which Garrett returned.

"Play in river?" he asked.

West almost laughed. It was cute the way his mind worked, but he needed to make sure that the kid understood. "The river's dangerous unless I'm with you. I don't want you anywhere near it unless you have a big person with you, okay?"

Garrett nodded solemnly, but West kinda figured he probably didn't understand. Still, didn't hurt to start teaching him now. If they were going to spend any amount of time here, he didn't want one of them accidentally falling down the bank and drowning in the river.

His body chilled at the thought, and he checked around to make sure all the kids were accounted for.

He counted three, and Gabriella was in her crib. All good.

The doorbell rang once more, and West was tempted to leave her outside.

"Because that crazy woman is going to make me walk to the door, isn't she?"

"Ray ray woman?"

His lip pulled back and down as he looked at Garrett. "I shouldn't have said that. I'll try to do better. Please don't you say it." Especially not in front of her.

His eyes crinkled at the thought of Poppy's outrage at hearing the boys call her that crazy woman.

It wouldn't make her mad. She'd just know exactly where the words came from, since the kids wouldn't have come up with that on their own.

He liked the idea and gave serious thought to encouraging Garrett to say it.

No, he couldn't do that to Garrett; it wasn't right. To encourage him to do something unkind just so he could get a charge out of Poppy's reaction.

Maybe he could get Garrett to call her Pollyanna though. That really wasn't mean.

With both boys in his arms, he strode down the hall, glancing into the bedroom where Minnie lay on his bed, in the same position she'd been when he'd walked back with Garrett and his pooped diaper underwear.

He slowed, listening for any sound from Gabriella. She'd already been up, eaten, and gone back to bed.

Or maybe that was just the fourth time she'd gotten up for the night. He wasn't sure if, after six o'clock, he should start counting that as morning waking or was that still nighttime waking?

Another thing he didn't think probably mattered to the rest of the world, but his world had kind of shrunk to his house, and the kids in it, and the woman on the bed.

And the sunshine at his door. He might have complained about her, but he could hardly wait to open it.

Setting Garrett down and adjusting the towel, he said, "Hold that for a minute. I'll get you dressed as soon as Craz…" He wasn't going to say that again. "Sorry. Soon as I let Miss Poppy in."

There. He was setting a good example. He should get a gold star or something. Or five minutes to go to the bathroom without a kid knocking on the door. That would be better than a gold star any day.

Oh, the things he didn't appreciate two weeks ago.

Opening the door, he said, "Good grief, Pollyanna. After the third time of ringing the—" He stopped midsentence.

The woman on his doorstep wasn't Poppy.

Definitely not Poppy. His brusque tone had made the wide-open eyes and eager expression crumple, and worse than anything, the eyes had started to fill with tears.

He had sisters, and he knew that girls' feelings could easily be hurt, but he hadn't meant anything by it. He hadn't even been talking to her. Hadn't meant to talk to her anyway.

The girl's eyes fluttered.

He recognized her from church, although he honestly hadn't paid much attention to her before. Was her name Paula? He wasn't sure.

"I'm sorry. I didn't mean to bother you." Her voice was timid, and she swallowed hard.

She was probably about his age. Maybe a little younger. Shy, he supposed, since she typically walked around with her head down, and he was pretty sure this wasn't the first time she'd apologized to him.

Now it was his turn.

"I'm sorry. I thought you were someone else."

"You can tell by the doorbell ringing who it is?" Her eyes brightened. "That's so cool! Is there like a video camera or something? I'd love to see it." She gave a timid smile while brushing her hair back and smoothing her hand down her shirt.

He shook his head. "No. I'd...I just thought someone else was going to be here today. I don't have a video camera." Or anything of the sort. "And I can't tell who's at the door by the way the doorbell rings. Honest."

Goodness. He felt like an idiot. Rather than being happy to see her, he found himself wondering how soon he could get her to go. Did he have to invite her in?

And where was Poppy?

"I brought the clothes the church collected for the kids. And..." She rocked her shoulders back and forth, her hands behind her back, and she shuffled a foot on the floor as her eyes went down. "I...I, uh, I can help you with the kids today. That's what I'm supposed to do."

"I don't suppose there's any pull-ups in that bag?"

Her eyes filled with panic, and her cheeks, already red, seemed to brighten even more. "I don't think so. It's just clothes."

An idea, so brilliant he almost smiled, came into his head. "You know I think I have the kids under control, but it's hard to get to the store. If I give you money, would you go get me a package of something called pull-ups? It's like disposable underwear, from what I understand."

Her eyes looked like open oil drums, and her mouth formed an "o" before she put her hand over top of it. She took a step back. "I had no idea you had problems like that."

Yeah, that served him right. For all the uncharitable thoughts that he'd been having about her. Because she wasn't Poppy.

"Not for me. For this guy." He jerked his head at Garrett who had the towel clutched around him, thankfully, because he wouldn't want to offend this lady's sensibilities, which seemed to be rather delicate, and stood grinning up at her. Yeah, something about being naked in a towel made a male grin. Good to see Garrett not only refused to wear Barbie doll pull-ups but had the male propensity for loving nakedness. There was hope for the kid after all.

"Oh." Now, not only were her cheeks bright red, her forehead had pinkened as well. "Oh. Of course." She spoke around the hand that was still over her mouth. "Of course. I'm so sorry. I'm sorry." Her head wagged back and forth. "Of course, they're not for you. That was really stupid of me. Sometimes, I just do stupid things. Sorry."

"Hey, lady. Look!" Garrett said, and he swung both ends of the towel wide open, exposing the lady's delicate sensibilities to naked little boy parts and upsetting her to the point that she took two quick steps backward, slipping off the porch and stumbling down the first step. A quick grab on the porch post kept her from falling backward down the stairs.

"Hey, careful."

"Oh, yes. I'm sorry. I will be more careful. So sorry about that. Really. I'm sorry."

"You can quit apologizing." West tried to temper the impatience in his tone. Man, he wished Poppy, with her sensible help and scoop of sunshine and get-it-done attitude, were here.

"Let me get my wallet." He didn't want her to leave and forget about the pull-ups.

He reached in his back pocket where he always kept his wallet, then he remembered he hadn't stuck it in this morning because it wasn't sitting on his dresser where it usually was. But the baby had been crying, and he hadn't thought too much more about it because then he'd had kids starving for breakfast, which he'd tried to make while feeding the baby, and then there'd been the spilled cereal, which of course had just had milk poured on it, and Trevor was crying because the cold milk landed on him, and Warren was crying because it'd been the last of the box of his favorite cereal, and West had wished he just made eggs because they seemed less controversial, but it was too late, and he wasn't sure whether it was safe to be cooking over the stove while feeding a baby anyway, and then the pooped underwear happened, and he hadn't even given his wallet another thought.

What kind of man didn't think about his wallet?

But now it came back to him. Poppy had his wallet.

Now what? He couldn't send this girl to the store to buy pull-ups for him without paying her.

But he had to do something to get her to go somewhere else, or he might end up stuck in the house with her all day. It was one thing to be stuck with Poppy, whom he could tease and pick on and who would take it without crying, and give it back to him, and make him wish that he could laugh...that was fine.

He didn't want to have to walk around on eggshells all day worried that he was going to offend this one. He might as well admit from the beginning that he was going to offend her.

And she was a nice girl. She didn't deserve to have to spend the day with him. It probably wasn't high on her list of things she wanted to do either.

"I'm sorry. Someone else has my wallet, and I just remembered." He would have thought Poppy would have made sure he got it back.

"I don't know if that's what this is, but Poppy seemed to be very insistent that I not allow anything to happen to it and hand it directly to you." The girl picked up the manila envelope that was lying on top of the big garbage bag that sat beside her. She handed it over.

Trevor clung to his neck as he opened the manila envelope. It felt thick enough and small enough that it could be his wallet sitting down there in the bottom of it.

There was a note, and he pulled that out first.

> West,
>
> I was going to make this ransom note, just to see if I could exhort money out of you for all the times you called me Pollyanna. However, you lucked out, because I've taken pity on you. You have your hands full with the kids and with Minnie.
>
> I'm sure you're worried about your wallet, however.

If getting it back makes you smile, be very careful, because I'm pretty sure we both know if you smile, a trapdoor opens up underneath your feet and you fall to China. Remember they're communist. And you probably wouldn't do very well in their system. Don't let those lips turn up.

Ever smiling (and always your opposite),

Poppy (Pollyanna to the dark people of this world)

West snorted. The corners of his lips trembled.

The little brat. Of course, she couldn't just give him his wallet back. She had to have some snide comments to go along with it.

He couldn't believe she wrote that kind of note though. Surely, she realized she didn't mention unicorns or rainbows one time.

Reaching in the manila envelope, he pulled out his wallet. He knew he didn't need to count the money in it. Pollyanna wouldn't take anything.

Pulling a twenty out, he handed it to Paula. "If you want to help me today, go to the store and buy as many pull-ups as that will buy."

Paula blinked several times like she wasn't sure exactly what he was asking her to do before she reached up and carefully took the money from him, and if he wasn't mistaken, she was extra careful not to brush his fingers.

Maybe she thought his bad attitude was contagious.

His thoughts weren't charitable. He was just frustrated because he had been looking forward to seeing Poppy and she wasn't here. He also wanted to answer her. It wasn't fair that she got the last laugh.

And then he remembered: he had her phone number.

"Do you need help carrying the clothes in?" Paula asked, and he thought she sounded almost hopeful. But that couldn't be right.

"No thanks. I'm good. These pull-ups are more important than clothes, to be honest."

She nodded quickly, her head bobbing up and down. "I'll get them. As many as I can. Really fast."

"Hey."

She'd already started off the porch, and she jerked to a stop, turning. "Yes?"

"If I don't answer the doorbell, just go ahead and set them in front of the door. I'll check after lunch."

Her eyes fell. He felt a little bad. Race and Penny wouldn't send anyone to him that wouldn't seriously be a help, but he kind of felt like he'd be better off doing this himself than constantly worrying about offending Paula. Or scaring her. Or upsetting her. Whatever happened when she got all red like that.

He felt bad about it, wished he could fix it, but he had the kids to deal with.

He wasn't fooling himself. He didn't want Paula, not because she was a pain, but because she wasn't Poppy.

He stepped back and closed the door, grinning down at Garrett who took his towel and spread his arms out, creating wings above his naked little body.

As he went sailing through the living room, yelling some kind of battle cry at the top of his lungs, West thought, what would happen if he just let the kid be naked? Would the poop fall out behind him? Or maybe that would help him remember to go to the potty?

Maybe they could make some kind of deal about it. He could be naked as long as he pooped in the pot.

Even if the poop fell out behind him, it would be easier to clean up if it were just lying on the floor rather than smashed into underwear and little boy butt.

He was gonna solve the problem. No doubt.

But first, pulling his phone out, he sent Poppy a text.

The trapdoor thing? It's not true.

He found the emoji button and selected a unicorn before hitting send.

Chapter Nine

*P*oppy looked at her phone and laughed.

Who would have thought West could make her laugh with a text?

It came at the perfect time.

"It's my professional opinion that your mother will never be able to live on her own again." The serious-looking man wearing a long white lab coat and holding an iPad stood beside Poppy looking through the one-way glass at where her mother stood staring out the window at the rolling green fields of Missouri while Hazel sat quietly at the child's desk behind her, her coloring book and crayons in front of her but her hands clasped on her lap, staring at the desk.

"We have Hazel interacting with other children, in a pre-K and a 4-K program, but a more normal home life would be better for her." The man clicked a couple of buttons on his iPad. "Your mother has agreed to this. She knows it's for the best. Especially now that she's on a suicide watch."

"I wish there was more I could do. It seems like she's worsened today because of seeing me."

"I think seeing you reminds her of the life she lost. That's the trouble right now. We can't get her to stop focusing on her loss and start thinking about the possibilities and opportunities of her future. She can't stop her downward spiral. Medication helps, but she needs to change her thinking pattern."

Poppy nodded. She knew exactly what the doctor was saying. It was what she had had to do in order to move past the tragedy that had claimed her family.

Several hours later, she held Hazel's hand as they walked down the walk, away from the long, low building that housed her mother and other people enrolled in the experimental program funded by private donors that her mother, by virtue of the depth of her tragedy, had earned a scholarship for.

Maybe she should have told Hazel they were coming back, but she didn't know if they actually were and she didn't want to lie to her sister.

All Hazel knew was that she was going to visit Poppy for a bit because Mommy was sad.

"It looks like you like to color," Poppy said, attempting again to draw her sister out. Her previous attempts had not been successful. The little girl was quiet. Exceptionally so.

She nodded but didn't speak.

"What's your favorite thing to do?"

The solemn little girl beside her lifted her shoulders, her hand limp in Poppy's, her little pink suitcase rolling behind them on the sidewalk.

She let the silence stand. She had time. There would be things she could do to form a bond between Hazel and her and develop a relationship.

A little pinch of fear went through her.

Any time the idea of a relationship forming went through her brain, it scared her. Because it reminded her of the pain of loss.

The almost unbearable pain of loss.

She had settled Hazel in a booster seat in the back of her car and pulled her phone out of her purse in order to get the GPS up when she saw West's text.

It made her smile again. In her mind, anything that made her smile after a morning like she'd had was valuable.

Maybe the man would think she was bothering him, but she didn't care. After all, he texted her first. So she adjusted her phone and typed her own message.

> You smiled just so you could prove me wrong, didn't you?

She hit send with a grin. Then she pulled the map app up, tapped in her address, got in, and started her car. It was going to be a long drive, and it could end up being an even longer night, although Hazel was hardly acting like anything was going to be a problem.

Poppy had never seen such a quiet, solemn little girl.

She hadn't wanted to get involved, hadn't wanted to risk her heart again, but Hazel was her sister, and she loved her. And the risk was worth it in order to try to help her own flesh and blood who'd already had so many bad things happen to her.

It was after dark when they arrived at Poppy's one-room efficiency apartment which she rented from the hardware store owner in front.

It wasn't much smaller than the apartment that Hazel had been sharing with her mother at the institute. Hazel's expression didn't change as she stood in the doorway and looked around.

They'd picked up some fast food on the way home, and Poppy threw the garbage away, giving Hazel a chance to look around. Her lack of interest was really concerning. Poppy had never met another four-year-old who smiled or talked less.

But the doctors at the institute hadn't seemed concerned, convinced that children are resilient and a new location would be just the thing.

Poppy wasn't always necessarily inclined to trust doctors, since, in her experience, real-world experience beat out book learning almost every time, and many doctors had the book learning down but not the actual experience.

Still, she wasn't going to discount them, and maybe a little faith was what she needed.

"If I draw some water, would you like to take a bath?" she asked, bracing herself for a shrug or no response.

But to her surprise, Hazel nodded. "I like to play in the bathtub."

Poppy tried to keep her mouth from dropping to the floor. That was the longest sentence Hazel had said all day. "Well, let's get you in there then."

"Do you have toys?"

The first question she'd asked without being prompted.

"I'll get some pots and pans out of the cupboard. We'll make our own toys."

Hazel didn't look convinced, but ten minutes later, she was happily playing in the bathtub with some measuring cups, wooden spoons, and several mixing bowls. A wire whisk and a hand-cranked eggbeater were also keeping her occupied.

Poppy hadn't quite seen a smile yet, but she figured it was coming.

Keeping the bathroom door open, she went out and grabbed her purse, pulling her phone out to put it on the charger.

That's when she saw West's new text and remembered that she'd seen he'd sent one while she was driving but hadn't stopped to read it.

She pulled it up now.

> Victory is sweet. (Come on over to the dark side.)

Her laugh was drowned out by splashing in the tub, and she walked into the bathroom holding her phone, putting the toilet seat down and sitting on it.

"Looks like you might be making pancakes for breakfast

tomorrow," she said as Hazel carefully used the eggbeater in a bowl half full of water.

"Uh huh," Hazel said, her face not quite as pinched as it had been earlier, although her lips had not turned up. "Blueberry pancakes."

"Oh. Blueberry are my favorite too. Are you going to share?"

The eggbeater stopped, and Hazel's eyes lifted, her face solemn. "Yes. I share."

"Maybe I can find some spaghetti sauce in the cupboard to put on the pancakes."

"Ugh," Hazel wrinkled her nose. "You don't put skettie sauce on pancakes. You need syrup."

"Well, I guess we'll have to make some syrup then. How do you do that?" Poppy said, fingering her phone and wondering if she might get a smile out of her sister tonight yet.

The narrow shoulders went up in a quick shrug. "You need a recipe book. It will tell you how."

"Maybe I can look it up on the Internet."

"The Internet lies."

Hmm. "It does about some things. You have to use your brain when you're using the Internet. But it probably tells us how to make syrup."

"Don't you have a recipe?"

"I suspect there isn't one for syrup. Probably we should buy it at the store. I can make peanut butter though. Are you sure you don't want that on your pancakes?"

"Ooo. That's gross like spaghetti sauce. Peanut butter is yucky on pancakes."

"How do you know? Have you tried it?"

Hazel's brows lowered, and her head shook slowly back and forth.

"Don't you think you should try it before you tell me you don't like it?"

"That just sounds yucky."

"Actually, what sounds yucky is pickles and pancakes. Especially pickles and blueberry pancakes. Pickles and strawberry pancakes might not be too bad."

"I like pickles."

"Then we'll have pickles and pancakes for breakfast in the morning."

"Can we have syrup too?"

"Maybe I can find some syrup."

That seemed to satisfy Hazel, and she poured the water from the pan she was working in into a measuring cup before pouring it into the other pan, carefully, like she was actually measuring it.

Poppy watched, her mind half on her sister, and ways to get her to smile, and half on West's text.

Hazel focused on pouring her water, so Poppy took a minute to send another text.

> Never. You might have won the battle, but read the back of the book. I win the war.

Maybe she was feeling a little smug over that text. More smug than she should be feeling, except it was West, and she knew he'd take it the way she meant it.

She was thinking about West, and she almost fell off the toilet when her phone buzzed in her hand. A call from Miss Penny.

"Hello?" she said, a little breathlessly, since the call had startled her.

"Hello, Poppy. I had something I wanted to ask you, but I also wanted to know how things went with your mother and Hazel today?"

Poppy gave her a brief summary of what the doctor had said about her mother and the fact that Hazel was with her now as she got up and walked out of the bathroom. She didn't want Hazel to hear and be upset.

After Poppy had finished, Penny didn't say anything for a bit.

Poppy ran her finger along the handle of the refrigerator, trying to keep out the thoughts that wanted to crowd into her brain.

Thoughts that were unhelpful. Like, why did this have to be her life? Why couldn't she have normal parents? A mom and a dad? Why did she have to be the one who had a tragedy? And why was it so, so hard to be positive?

"So, you have Hazel for now. Are you keeping her?" Penny asked a little hesitantly.

"It looks like it. I guess we just kind of left it up in the air. When I tried to talk to Mom, all she did was cry. But the doctor told me that she was willing to sign away guardianship to me." She hesitated, unsure whether or not she could admit this. "I'm not sure I want it."

She could hear Miss Penny's deep sigh all the way through the phone.

"I can't say I understand. I don't think there are too many people in the world who could understand. Not too many have been through tragedy like you. But I can see where that thought is coming from. And I can also see where you might feel guilty because it feels selfish. I can't say that I wouldn't do the same thing and feel the same way if I were in your shoes. I just want you to know there's no judgment here."

Her words, though they weren't words of approval necessarily, made Poppy feel so much better. Like a light had come on in her soul, shining away the darkness that seemed to have descended there since she had left the institute.

It hadn't been entirely darkness. The little laugh she'd shared with West had kept it from being pitch black.

Suddenly, she couldn't wait to read his text.

But she didn't try to do that while she was talking to Miss Penny.

"Thank you. Even though I know the right thing to do is to open my heart up again, if that's what it is, it's just scary and hard and I don't even feel like I have a whole heart. It feels crumpled and wrinkled and battered. Permanently."

"We serve a God who is in the business of healing." Then Penny grunted. "That sounded so trite and superficial even though it's true,

I guess we say it often enough that sometimes those words lose their meaning. Please think about it, because I know you believe it."

"I do. I don't even know if that's the problem. I just...I've worked so hard at not letting the sadness and the darkness beat me. I see my mom, and I want more than anything not to be like that. And for me, having Hazel here is like my mom seeing me. Hazel looks exactly like my sisters Rachel and Esther. It's all I can do to call her by her name instead of theirs."

"It's hard to live with a ghost."

"Yeah." Especially when that ghost felt like they were sticking a knife in your heart every time a person looked at them.

"Well, not to change the subject, although it definitely is a subject change, I was really calling to see if you could run these pull-ups out to West tomorrow. Paula had gone and gotten them, but for some reason, she didn't want to deliver them to West's farm."

"That's because West is stygian. Paula was scared."

Poppy knew Penny would love that, even though West was her son. Penny and Race were no stranger to West's and hers light and dark banter.

Paula wasn't exactly known for her fearless personality, either. That might have been Poppy at one time.

"That could be it," Penny said with a laugh in her voice. "But she also had to start her shift at the diner. Let's go with that."

"Everybody has their narrative to describe the world. Let's just agree to disagree."

Their laughter mingled, and then Poppy, still smiling, said, "I think it would be nice to take a ride with Hazel tomorrow. Although I haven't watched the weather lately. What will the storm be doing?"

Oddly, Penny seemed to hesitate, then stumble, before she said, "Actually, I think it's supposed to begin tomorrow. Or maybe the rain is supposed to start tonight. And then maybe it's supposed to end in snow. I've just heard glimpses of the weather forecast."

"Oh. Okay."

Maybe Penny was stumbling because she wasn't confident in her forecast.

"I promised Hazel pancakes for breakfast, but we'll do it after that."

"Sounds good. I'll drop the bag off at the diner."

"Perfect."

They chatted a bit more before hanging up.

Immediately, Poppy started walking to the bathroom, pulling her texting app up along with West's text.

It surprised her.

> After the day I had, I think I'll let you win.
> Good night.

She stood in the bathroom doorway, cognizant that Hazel was still happily playing with the bowls and eggbeater, while her heart sank.

West seemed so indestructible. So strong. Like nothing could get to him.

It hurt her heart that he sounded so defeated in that text. Probably after dealing with four small children and a woman who was dying with cancer all day, it would be enough to wear anyone down. She just hadn't thought that of West.

But they didn't exactly have the kind of relationship where she could be serious with him and offer true words of encouragement and help. But maybe she could send something whimsical. Something that would give him a little lift at the end of his hard day.

> Hang in there, Dracula. The light is coming, tomorrow, in fact, and I'm bringing hope and cheer in the form of three packs of pull-ups.

She'd barely made it to the shelf to grab a towel for Hazel when her phone dinged. She wasn't expecting an answer that fast.

> Bring your smile. I need it.

Chapter Ten

*I*t was 10 o'clock, and he hadn't served breakfast yet.

Gabriella at least had eaten. Twice. He was working on the third time. It seemed like everything he did, he did with the baby in the crook of his arm.

Garrett had pooped his pants twice, and the second time, West just left his underwear off. So the kid was running around naked. Yesterday when he left his underwear off, Garrett hadn't gone to the bathroom at all outside of the actual bathroom.

Five minutes after he put his pants on, they were wet.

West believed himself to be kind of thick at times, but he could definitely see a pattern there.

"Is it ready yet? I'm hungry."

West made a mental note to invest fifty dollars in boxed cereal the next time he was near a grocery store.

He had a few chickens out in the barn, enough that he enjoyed eggs for breakfast every morning and had a few to share on Sundays at church.

But he hadn't made it out to the barn to gather the eggs lately, not to mention it was a lot harder to cook eggs than it was to dump something in a bowl and hand it to a kid.

Less stressful, too, since the kids seemed to prefer the sugar in a bowl over the eggs.

He probably would have to accept that, except going to the barn for eggs beat going to the store for cereal any day.

A crash broke through his thoughts. One that sounded like a chair being flipped over and landing on the floor in the dining room. A three-second pause of complete silence, and then Trevor started to scream.

West put the fork down that he was using to scramble the eggs and walked into the room to make sure lives were not in danger. It had been about two weeks, and he'd figured out that crying, no matter how bad, meant the kid that was crying hadn't died.

Crying was good.

Sure enough, he could see from the doorway that Trevor was already trying to clamber to his feet. So obviously, he wasn't dead, and it didn't look like anything was broken either.

Not on the kid. Not on the chair.

Wins all around.

West started walking forward to right the chair and pick the kid up, then he decided there was no point in righting the chair, since it would probably just get knocked over again.

He figured he might as well let Trevor cry it out, too, since his cries already seemed to be less loud and angry.

He supposed, even if he had a parenting handbook, he wouldn't use it anyway. But he was pretty sure it didn't hurt kids to cry.

Movement on the other side of the doorway caught his eye, and he realized Minnie was standing there. With the white t-shirt he'd given her to wear, since she'd sweated through her nightgown and he'd not gotten the laundry done, she looked like a skeleton wearing a white sheet. A short white sheet, since it only came to mid-thigh.

A ghost of a smile kept her face from looking too spectral.

"Sometimes if you leave them alone, they calm themselves

down," she said, with a glance at Trevor, who had stopped crying and was trying to set his dump truck back on its wheels.

"I think I had just figured that out. Two weeks ago, that would have been a revelation for me."

"I'm so sorry." Her eyes closed, and her hand reached out like she needed the support of the doorway in order to stay on her feet. "I should have never come. I obviously have made your life miserable."

"Not miserable. This is good for me." He figured the words were true, even if he didn't really want to believe them and would prefer not to have this "good" thing happen to him.

Her head shook while her eyes stayed closed. "I was selfish. I tried to think of the best person that I could, someone that I could see being good with my kids. And you are the only one that came to my mind. I should have talked to you about it before I just showed up. And now..." She took a breath, like talking had robbed her of everything, including the ability to breathe. "I'm too weak and tired to try to come up with a plan B."

"No need for plan B. I'm here. I'm actually starting to like these rug rats. Most of the time."

He eyed Garrett who had found a towel from somewhere and had stretched it over his shoulders, naked except for the wings that spread out behind him as he ran around between the living room and the hall behind his mom, bursting out into the dining room.

Thankfully, seeing his chubby little legs churning under the towel made Minnie smile. At least her lips turned up.

Before he could say anything more, the doorbell rang, followed by a firm knock on the door, followed by the door opening.

Poppy, her face lit up like Fourth of July fireworks, with a light spring in her step, holding the hand of an unfamiliar-looking little girl, strode confidently into his house, closing the door behind her.

"Good morning, everyone!" she said, the Pollyanna in her personality filling the room like helium in a balloon.

"It's morning. I'll give you that," he said, realizing he was making a deliberate effort to keep from returning her smile. He was pretty sure it wasn't the pull-ups in her hand but rather the memory of her text from last night that made his mouth want to turn up.

Sure enough, she lifted the white plastic bag, and it crinkled cheerfully. Frankly, that was the first time in his life he ever considered a bag cheerful. Figured it would be one that Poppy was holding.

"Look what I have. And if you want them, you're going to have to smile for them."

She gave him a superior look, which included a raised eyebrow and pressed-up lips, and then as her head turned, she froze.

"I'm sorry. I've spoken to you a bit, but I'm not sure we were properly introduced. You must be Minnie. I'm Poppy."

As those words were tumbling out of her mouth, she had started toward Minnie like she was going to give her a hug when she seemed to hesitate.

Her smile dimmed slightly, and her brows seemed almost scrunched together. Something definitely bothered her.

Interesting that he could see those little signs, but he didn't want to guess what they could mean. Definitely didn't want to admit that maybe he had been watching Poppy more than he thought or that he was interested in her reactions.

Poppy's gaze skittered to him before they went back to Minnie, and then her step lengthened, her posture became bold once again, and she closed the rest of the distance between Minnie and herself, wrapping her arms around Minnie.

"I got to spend some time with your children, and they are so sweet. It's impossible not to fall in love with them."

Her words made Minnie smile as her translucent hands came up and weakly patted Poppy's strong back.

Lifting her hands made his T-shirt ride up Minnie's matchstick legs. Could that have been what gave Poppy pause? Minnie in his T-shirt?

"It's so good to see you up. It's raining like crazy out there, and the river is really up. We're supposed to get a lot of snow, too."

Poppy stepped back. "I thought maybe I could help with lunch, and I can definitely get these pull-ups out. Looks like Garrett can use one."

Her words were peppy and full of vitality and energy that he just wasn't feeling after being up with Gabriella most of the night.

"As long as Garrett's naked, he does his business in the potty." His words sounded defensive, probably because they were.

"So, you've rewritten the manual on potty training. Cool beans." She held up the bag again. "Should I return these to the store? I understand you paid for them. If you don't need them, maybe you'd like your money back?"

"Very funny. Don't be hasty. Just set the bag down, back slowly away from it, and no one gets hurt."

Like he figured, her eyes crinkled, and her face wreathed in a grin as she stepped farther away from Minnie.

"I take it that was a yes that you want me to start cooking lunch?"

"Breakfast. We haven't gotten breakfast down yet."

Her eyebrows shot up, and her eyes fluttered for a second or two. "It's, like, almost 11 o'clock. You haven't had breakfast?"

"Some of us have been busy this morning." His eyes met hers across the room, and he thought about the text he'd sent last night. Of course, he couldn't know what she was thinking, but he could almost imagine that text going through her head too.

He'd been tired, and she caught him in a weak moment. It was a text he normally would never have sent.

He made a mental note to not text at night when he was tired and felt defeated and discouraged.

Still, as much as he regretted it, he didn't feel judgment, and he didn't feel like she was going to make fun of him. If anything, he felt compassion in her gaze, and commiseration. Maybe she was light and he was dark, but there was something in her that drew him. And he was thinking that maybe she didn't hate him quite as much as he thought she had.

His heart stirred, and something warm and sweet seemed to coat the inside of his ribs.

He pulled his gaze away, trying to focus on all the things that needed to be done and not on the woman who'd just burst into his house and brightened it by her very presence.

He was never going to get his crops in the ground or his equipment serviced, and speaking of, he hadn't even ordered seed.

He bit back the irritation as Garrett, still naked, still holding the towel like wings, ran by again.

He didn't want to lose his farm, and he needed to get his work done, but these kids had wormed their way into his heart in just a small amount of time. It was scary, honestly, but his heart also felt beautifully full.

His eyes slid to Poppy, then to the little girl that still clutched her hand, a serious look on her face.

"Who's that?" He nodded at the little girl.

"I'm sorry. This is my sister, Hazel. I brought her back with me yesterday after visiting my mom. She's going to be with me for a while, and I was hoping that she would have fun playing with Garrett and Warren and Trevor."

"I don't want to play," the little girl whispered.

West's eyes narrowed. A child that didn't want to play? He hadn't been around many children, but he couldn't remember his siblings and him ever not wanting to play. That was pretty much the goal of their childhood. To play.

"You don't have to, sweetheart," Poppy said easily. "They haven't had any breakfast, so you can come out and help me make it."

"Is that a baby?" the little girl said, looking at Gabriella whom West had put over his shoulder. He patted her back carefully.

"It is," he said, not waiting for Poppy to answer. "Do you like babies?"

Hazel's head went up and down.

"Want to come over here so you can see her?" He lifted his gaze to Minnie, who had tears in her eyes.

"She's so precious. I was worried about Gabriella with three older brothers and no sisters." She blinked, as though trying to keep her tears from running down her cheeks. Her face turned to Poppy. "Thank you so much for bringing her."

As though just talking had exhausted her, she seemed to lean forward a little bit, and Poppy hurried over and put her arm around her shoulders.

"Would you like to sit down?" Poppy asked gently.

"I need to get ready to go. Penny is picking me up to take me to my appointment this afternoon," Minnie said, but she swayed, like she was going to fall.

"I'll help you." Poppy threw a look over her shoulder at West, who had knelt down and waited for Hazel, who had stopped a good three or four feet away from him, afraid to close the distance.

Her eyes were bright though, as she looked at Gabriella, and her little body leaned forward while one hand came up, almost like she was going to reach out to touch.

West and Poppy shared a look before Poppy turned.

He had sisters, sure, but he'd been more concerned about teasing them than figuring them out. He had no idea what was in her eyes, gratitude maybe. Concern, definitely. And maybe a little fear.

He wondered about that last.

But he also thought...he thought there might have been, not pride exactly, but some kind of emotion that was directed at him. A positive emotion.

He most definitely had never considered Poppy as anyone of interest to him. But he couldn't deny the feeling like he was being pulled toward her had gotten stronger.

Chapter Eleven

"You can come closer." He tried to make his voice carefully kind as he directed his words to Hazel.

It wasn't a natural sound for him. He'd never been around kids, except for Minnie's for the last two weeks, and they were boys.

Except for Gabriella of course, who hadn't needed him to talk to her, just to feed her and change her and hold her in the night while she cried.

Hazel was a completely different story.

He would almost say he loved the boys. Funny, it had only taken two weeks for that to happen, and he would protect them, sure. But somehow, the protective feeling was stronger toward Hazel, which was really odd considering that he'd just met her ten minutes ago.

"We'll wait until your mom comes back, but if she says yes, you could probably sit down and hold her, too."

"Really?" Hazel's eyes glowed, and her lips tugged up.

"Really."

"She's not my mom. She's my sister."

"Yeah. Forgot."

"Does the baby live here?"

He almost said "for now," but he stopped himself just in time. He didn't know what the story was on Hazel, but what he knew of Gabriella and her brothers' story, it wasn't a good one.

A child deserved permanence in their life, not a "for now" answer that wasn't an answer.

"Yes."

Her hair was a little wet, probably from the rain outside, and as he thought about it, Poppy's had been wet too.

It just added to her sparkle. Another woman might have looked like a drowned rat. But somehow it made Poppy glow even more.

"Can I touch her?"

Gabriella burped, a sound that maybe would have been cute if it hadn't been accompanied by what seemed like at least twice as much liquid as he had put into her running down his shirt.

"You sure can. Watch out, she might get you too."

Hazel's eyes widened, then, to his surprise, she giggled.

The solemn little girl that had been standing beside her sister five minutes ago disappeared, and she looked much more normal to West.

That's the way a child should act. Giggles. It was also normal, he supposed, for girls to be interested in babies.

Or maybe it was just something new.

Anyway, none of Gabriella's brothers seemed to pay much attention to her. West couldn't remember ever giving a baby a thought in his life before, certainly not when he was a kid.

Hazel came closer, within arm's length, and touched Gabriella's back.

"She's warm."

"Just like you are."

That made Hazel's brows go down, and she used the hand that was touching Gabriella to touch her cheek.

"My cheek is cold."

"Touch your stomach."

He turned Gabriella around, so once Hazel had touched her own stomach, she could feel Gabriella's stomach.

Hazel lifted her shirt just a little and put her hand on her stomach.

"I'm warm, too," she said, wonder in her voice, like she'd never stopped to discover that she was warm before.

West couldn't help smiling at the dawn of knowledge on her face. He couldn't remember ever figuring out that he was warm. But it must be something everyone learned at one point. It was weird to see it happening. Weird...and special.

Movement caught his eye. He looked over to see both Warren and Garrett putting their hands on their stomachs, the latter having dropped his towel cape-wings.

Trevor, who probably didn't understand what was going on, exactly, lifted his shirt and put his hand on his stomach too.

It didn't surprise him at all when the boys gathered around and put their hands on Gabriella's little belly. He didn't even have to remind them to be gentle.

"We're all warm," Warren said, his surprise endearing.

A shadow fell across them, and West looked up.

"I'm impressed. I think you just taught everybody something," Poppy said, laughter in her voice, although he didn't think that she was making fun of him necessarily. Just laughing along with him, because it was adorable that all the kids had just discovered that they were warm.

"When is she going to walk?" Hazel asked, taking her hand from Gabriella's stomach and trailing a finger down her bare legs and touching her toes.

"Probably not until next year this time," West said, liking how Hazel was so gentle with the baby. And so in awe of her.

He looked up at Poppy, struggling not to get lost in her gaze. "I told Hazel I'd ask if it would be okay if she holds the baby."

Poppy nodded. "I definitely think she could, with supervision." She put a hand on Hazel's head and ruffled her hair just a little. "I think when she gets comfortable with her, she should be able to do it on her own, but probably not today."

Hazel's chest puffed out like an adult's chest might have if they had been told they'd won the lottery. He kinda thought for a four-year-old girl, maybe holding a baby *was* like winning the lottery. At least for a girl like Hazel.

"You want me to help with the baby and Hazel? Or would you like me to get some food ready?"

"I'm hungry," Warren said, just in case they'd forgotten.

"Me too," Garrett echoed.

"I knew you were hungry," Poppy said, looking at Garrett. "You've already eaten your clothes." She gave Warren a warning glance. "You'd better be careful, he might start on yours next."

The boys giggled, and West had to fight again to keep his own lips from twitching up. She was silly enough to appeal to boys, and she hadn't even gotten to bodily noises and passing gas at either end. The boys would probably be rolling on the floor if she started on that.

He just hoped he had the self-control not to join them there.

She scooped Garrett up and patted Warren's shoulder.

Putting her forehead on Garrett's and wiggling it back and forth, she said, "Where are your clothes, my child?"

Her tone was just goofy enough to make Garett grin with all of his teeth showing. His little narrow shoulders went up and down and up and down.

"For some reason, he goes in the potty if he doesn't have any clothes on," West mumbled, feeling stupid. What kind of person let a kid run around naked? That wasn't something that was done in polite society.

"I believe you already mentioned your newfangled way of potty training. It probably also makes it easier if you don't have to scrape poop off underwear."

She tilted her head toward him while keeping her forehead

against Garrett's, who seemed to be pushing on her and turning the whole forehead thing into a competition.

Typical boy.

Their eyes caught, and it took him a couple of seconds to even think about replying. She didn't seem to be yelling at him for letting the kid run around naked. Not like a normal person might have. In fact, she kinda acted like it was an okay idea.

"Easier isn't always better," he said.

Somehow, his dad's comment that he heard a million times growing up as a kid came into his head at that time.

"If you had four small children dumped on your lap, and you're just trying to survive, I'm sorry, but easier is better."

He almost thought she might have winked at him before she turned her head back and ground it into Garrett's. He seemed to be pushing with all his little might with his head against hers.

"If you two boys want to help me mix up some pancakes, you can."

She slipped her head away, and Garrett's head surged forward, bopping on her shoulder before he pulled back, blinking.

She lowered her head at him. "But you, sir, at least need to have a pull-up on. We can't have naked cooks in the kitchen."

"I'm naked. I'm all naked." He giggled, like it was funny.

"How about we just have a naked top and a not naked bottom?"

"I can help?" He seemed to want to make sure of that before he agreed to any type of covering. West almost smiled.

"You sure can." Her brow scrunched up like she was going to ask a very deep question. "Can you crack eggs?"

Garrett's head went up and down, big and deep.

Poppy's head tilted. "Have you ever cracked eggs before?"

Garrett's head paused for just a moment before it started going back and forth just as big and wide.

"That's what I thought." She grinned and looked down at Warren. "Have you ever cracked eggs?"

"I dropped one on the floor once. That one cracked." Warren's lips didn't even move up; the kid was serious.

"Let's not count that one," Poppy said, her face just as serious. "I think anything that ends up on the floor doesn't get counted." Maybe she added that last bit when she saw how Warren's face fell when she discounted his "experience" in cracking eggs.

"I guess that means you and I are on baby-watching duty," he said to Hazel, who had not stopped touching Gabriella's legs and feet and rubbing her hand softly and carefully over her head.

"Can I hold her?"

West looked again at Poppy; she'd adjusted Garrett and had dug one-handed into the bag that contained the pull-ups.

She nodded her head at his look, and he said, "I'm pretty sure that everything that you do with children requires you to be skilled at working with just one hand."

She laughed. "I hadn't ever thought of that, but I'm sure you're right. Sometimes, I think a secondary skill is being able to work with your teeth. I had a sister who could tie a knot in a cherry stem in her mouth." Her voice trailed off, and she moved the hand that was under Garrett around and started seriously digging in the bag, suddenly focused on getting a pull-up like that was the single most important thing she would ever do with her life.

Chapter Twelve

"I didn't know you had another sister," West said to Poppy as he stood up and held his hand out for Hazel. If Poppy were going to be working in the kitchen, he'd go on out with her and have Hazel hold the baby out there.

He didn't question why he wanted to be where Poppy was.

Her head shook, and she lifted her shoulder without looking at him. "It was a long time ago."

"I'm pretty sure once you have a sister, you always have a sister. I've got five siblings. And things happened a long time ago, but I still have five siblings."

She managed to take a pull-up out of the bag, and in an act he thought was probably deliberate, she turned her back on him, bending over and setting Garrett down on the floor.

She held the pull-up so he could step into it.

Her head lifted. "I never even thought to ask. We do have eggs, correct?"

She had totally disregarded his question about her siblings. He supposed a nicer person would just let the subject drop.

People didn't usually accuse him of being nice.

"So, we're gonna pretend you don't have a sister? Even though you just now mentioned her?"

"That's right. I have Hazel."

"She wasn't the sister you were talking about."

Poppy ignored him, pulling the pull-up on Garrett until it was snug around his waist.

"Was she?" He wasn't going to let her ignore him.

"All right, Garrett. You ready to help?"

He let go of Hazel's hand and put his fingers on Poppy's arm. Her head swiveled up, and one look at her face had him taking a step back.

He'd never seen that look on her before. Nothing even close. Happiness. Light. Joy. Peace. All that was part of Poppy's Pollyanna personality. But now her eyes were squinted, and her lips pursed, and if a heartache had an image, it was stamped on her face.

"Please don't," she whispered. Not angry, just...

He wasn't even sure what the emotion was, but it was obvious that she'd been hiding something. Covering it with her happy façade.

That wasn't being fair. Maybe she'd chosen to be happy, and he scratched her too deep.

Whatever it was he'd done, the look on her face made his heart feel the same way. Sharp pain cut through, and his stomach pulled in, making him want to hunch over and definitely making him feel ashamed. He hadn't wanted to make her feel bad.

"Sorry."

She'd not been expecting an apology. That was clear from the way her eyes widened. Then they closed as she seemed to struggle with herself.

He still held Gabriella in one arm, but he was tempted, more tempted than he'd ever been, to take a step and wrap his other arm around Poppy.

She looked like she needed the support.

He hardly doubted his support would be welcome.

"Don't be. It's not your fault. I just can't talk about it."

"I was pushing you on purpose. I didn't realize how deeply your feelings ran. Sorry." He let out a breath. "I complained for years that your smile is annoying. But it's not, and I want it back. Please?" He hesitated, unsure whether he could tease her. He might have lost that right. He wouldn't have even said he had it. But he realized now, part of their banter had been because they were so comfortable with each other.

This new discovery of his, that there was more to Poppy than just some unicorns and rainbows, lollipops and happiness, had changed things for him. The fact that he'd crashed through the rainbows and lollipops might have taken his rights away.

But he wasn't going to give up. Not without trying.

"Do I need to tickle you? You look like the kind of girl who would be extremely ticklish."

Yeah, her lips curved. "I am. And if you start to tickle me, I can't guarantee that you're going to get breakfast." She looked at Garrett and then at Warren. "Although I will still feed the boys. As long as they don't join in and gang up on me."

"I like to tickle people," Garrett said.

"Tickle wars are fun. Garrett and I do it all the time," Warren said, standing so that he could see between the two of them, his eyes going back and forth, as though watching adults converse was a new experience for him.

"I've noted your position. And adjusted my intentions to wait until after breakfast before I begin tickling you," West said.

"Maybe I'll offer to watch the children after we eat so you can go outside and get something done." Her eyes went to the window. A wrinkle formed in her forehead. "Although it's pouring out there. This was supposed to be the storm of the century, but as you can see, it's all rain, and I highly doubt we're actually going to get the snow they called for."

"And even if we do, it's not going to lie on the ground."

"Exactly. Although we really are supposed to get a lot of rain. But

I don't think we need to worry about flooding, not in town, because Mistletoe is on a hill, and there's not really any low ground between here and there."

"No, you're right. If this storm does what they say it's going to, there are a lot of places in the state that are going to be dealing with flooding, but Mistletoe is not one of them. We're good on that end. If you don't mind, I actually will take you up on watching the kids for a while after lunch."

"It's contingent on whether or not you tickle me." She lifted her shoulder like it didn't matter to her. "The choice is all yours."

"You might think that's an easy choice, but the tickling is actually very tempting."

She grunted a laugh and scooped Garrett back up, taking one step before she froze. Looking around frantically, she gasped and turned wide eyes to him. "Where's Trevor? Have you seen him? He was just here with me, wasn't he? Where'd he go?"

West wasn't sure where her panic was coming from. The kid was around somewhere. Probably. He turned in a circle. "He was just here a couple of minutes ago." He looked at Warren. "Have you seen your brother?"

In his experience, when it came to the three boys, Warren was the most knowledgeable of them with anything sibling related.

Maybe he should ask Warren for advice on his crops. Warren always seemed to have all the answers. He was definitely much more knowledgeable with Gabriella than West was.

"He was in the bathroom."

The slight edge of panic that had pulled him, mostly because of the panic that Poppy seemed to be in, eased, and he actually felt like smiling. He turned to Poppy.

"Maybe he's potty training himself." His eyes went to Garrett, who had both arms around Poppy's neck and was digging his forehead into her cheek. "Garrett. I'm thinking you might be able to learn a lesson or two from your brother about excreting your bodily fluids in the proper place."

Garrett's head turned toward him. His little eyes looked confused.

Poppy didn't smile. "I wouldn't be too smug. When a kid disappears, and it's quiet? There's always a mess at the end of that."

"I think you're borrowing trouble," West said casually, interested that their position seemed to flip.

Poppy was supposed to be the eternal optimist, and he was the gloom-and-doom guy.

Poppy's attention had already gone to Warren. "Where's the bathroom?"

Warren pointed in the general direction.

"Lead me, please," Poppy said, her words clipped and short.

"Sure. Can I still help with breakfast?"

"Of course, you can. It's just going to be delayed a little more than it already has been." She lifted an eye to West, irony on her face. She'd given him a hard time because breakfast hadn't been served yet, but nothing had happened so far on her watch, either, in that direction.

Poppy followed on Warren's heels as he walked to the bathroom.

West held out his hand, and Hazel looked at it with quiet contemplation before she took it and they followed Poppy and Warren.

He fully expected to see Trevor sitting on the toilet doing whatever it was two-year-olds did on the toilet, hopefully putting all the gunk inside of him safely in its depths. If he had as much goop inside him as Garrett seemed to, it was going to take a while to get it all out.

West had had no idea that a body so little could produce so much waste. Toxic waste.

"Oh my goodness," Poppy said as she halted just inside the bathroom door.

Her hand went to her throat, and her breathing seemed to stop.

West reminded himself not to squeeze Hazel's hand when his own wanted to fist. His breathing deepened and sped up, along with his heartbeat. Like they were running away, although he had no idea where they were going.

Trevor stood in front of the toilet, his shirt off along with his pants.

That didn't necessarily shock West. He knew the boy could take his own clothes off.

What did shock him was that the discarded clothes were in the toilet, on top of what looked like an entire roll of toilet paper which had been unwound and stuffed into the toilet bowl. Basically, the toilet looked like it had become a confetti gun, jammed with toilet paper, with the two-year-old's clothes sitting on top.

"I had actually been dreaming about the kid sitting on the toilet and pooping in it. I'm hoping now that entire dream is wrong."

Basically, he was saying he sure as shooting hoped the toilet water was "clean." Because he was pretty sure he was going to be cleaning that mess up.

"Trevor. You're bad. You're in a lot of trouble," Warren said, his hands on his hips and his head shaking.

He turned and looked at the adults behind him. The look on his face was apprehensive, like he wasn't sure how the big people in his life were going to react to this latest development. There was also a bit of superiority there. Like, at least this time, he wasn't involved, and he knew *he* wasn't in trouble.

Trevor, on the other hand, had not yet realized that what he had done had been so egregiously bad that the wrath of God was about to descend upon him at any second.

Frustration and anger clogged up West's throat. How could a kid who couldn't even string three words together, who could barely stack two blocks without knocking them down, make such a huge mess?

He wanted to grab the kid by the scruff of the neck and toss him into a corner while at the same time he wanted to force the kid to stick his own hands in the water, which he didn't seem to have had any problem with because his hands were shiny wet, and clean everything up.

West certainly didn't want to have to do it.

"All right. Looks like breakfast is going to be even later than we thought." The cheerfulness that defined Poppy was loud and strong in her voice.

"How can you sound like that? This is a disgusting mess... Oh, never mind. I know how. Because I have to clean it up."

It was his house, after all. And he knew his words were mean and petty and angry and frustrated, but he couldn't help himself. Seriously? This was not what he signed up for. He hadn't signed up for anything. Someone had forged his signature.

This mess was a very good Exhibit A on why he didn't want to have children.

Not that he had ever decided to line up exhibits, but if he were, this would definitely be at the forefront. Along with the pooped underwear.

Raising kids was nothing but going from one mess to another cleaning them up.

Poppy smiled, almost benignly. "What if you take the girls, and Garrett and Warren, and go get me a big garbage bag so I can put this stuff in it." She looked around. "Do you have rubber gloves somewhere?"

"No. I don't."

"Maybe we can invest in a pair. They come in handy." Her grin was lopsided, and it eased some of the tightness in his chest.

This was not funny, it wasn't a happy moment, but he could see how her reaction was a little better than his.

It made him want to be better. Mostly.

So he swallowed. "We'll get you a garbage bag. Do you need anything else?"

"Maybe we can get a basket of dirty laundry that needs to be washed and throw this outfit on top of it. We can get it in the washer and get moving on that."

Laundry wasn't even something he had tried to keep up with. It seemed overwhelming to do everything else. Clean clothes hadn't seemed important when he was trying to keep the kids from starving to death.

"I'm on it."

"Thanks."

Their eyes met across the kids, and despite the mess and beyond the surface irritations, he could feel something stirring in his chest. Something that had been preceded by the warmth and the odd tightening, and now it grew bigger, expanding his heart and making it thump low and slow, and shifting the way he had thought about himself, and her, and even the world between them.

It was scary.

He hated feeling afraid. So he fought the feeling. It wasn't what he wanted. Although the pull was tempting.

Somehow, he knew being with Poppy would be fun. And right there, that represented a huge shift in his thinking.

Being with Poppy?

Where did that idea come from?

He pulled his gaze away and shook his head. Not going to happen. She had some kind of weird thing going on with her sister, whatever that was, and he had enough junk in his past to fill a barge.

If only he could ship it somewhere like Antarctica.

Chapter Thirteen

It took forty-five minutes to clean up the toilet mess. A good pair of rubber gloves would have been very welcome.

She'd been at the hospital visiting new moms, and she'd seen the samples of formula, the packs of diapers, and even baby bags and clothes that were showered on the proud new parents.

Parents were not even allowed to leave the hospital without a car seat.

Personally, she felt parenting without rubber gloves should be illegal.

Still, the mess was cleaned, the toilet scrubbed, and Trevor had been dealt with.

He was little, and he was going through a hard thing with his mom and having lost his dad, but she had no intention of ever cleaning up a mess of that proportion instigated by Trevor again.

Probably Gabriella would do the same thing at some point. All kids seemed to.

But she was pretty sure Trevor understood that it wasn't to happen again.

West seemed to be a little more concerned about keeping track of the children as well.

Maybe by unspoken agreement, they'd both reached to shut the door as they were leaving the bathroom.

Their hands touched, and they shared a smile. And she'd made an interesting discovery.

West was gorgeous when he smiled.

That was a discovery, but it wasn't the biggest one.

The big discovery was, when West smiled, it made her heart do somersaults.

That was unexpected. And disconcerting. And not entirely welcome.

It felt good. It'd made her hand want to turn in, her fingers to trail across his palm and his wrist.

Not that she had done such a thing. Of course not. But it made her want to.

An entirely new desire that she wasn't quite sure what to do with.

She was certain, though, it wasn't welcome.

Regardless, the mess was cleaned, and now they were back in the kitchen. Garrett stood on a chair, Warren stood beside her, and Trevor sat on the counter.

As long as she was here, Trevor wasn't leaving her side.

West had Hazel in a chair. Hazel was in heaven, with Gabriella in her arms.

Love swelled in her chest for her sister. She didn't know what to do about her mom, wasn't sure there was anything she *could* do, and wished things were different, but she could say with her whole heart and soul she was thrilled that her little sister was staying with her and that she got to spend some time with her.

She wasn't entirely comfortable with the knowledge that there was pain ahead. In fact, she couldn't think about it, or it scared her.

But yeah. She loved her sister.

"Let me. Let me." Garrett held his hand out for the egg that she'd just taken out of the bowl West had set on the table counter when she'd asked about eggs.

A quick look in the refrigerator hadn't yielded any egg cartons. She hadn't considered looking for her eggs in a bowl.

Apparently, he had chickens in the barn, and these were gathered from there.

West had never struck her as the egg-gathering type, but appearances were deceiving, apparently.

"What we're going to do is crack it into this bowl first. That way if we get any shells in it, we can scrape them out. Eggshells in pancakes are yucky."

She wrinkled her nose, and Garrett stuck out his tongue.

"And we can also make sure it's a good egg." She didn't think about her childhood on the farm very often, deliberately, but she knew from experience that sometimes an egg got missed for a week or so, and it wasn't any good when it finally did get found and taken to the house. No point in ruining the entire batter because she cracked a bad egg directly into it.

"Now, I'll hand you the egg in a second, but I want you to listen first. What you're going to do is gently tap it on the corner of the counter until the shell cracks, and then you're going to put both thumbs into the crack and pull it apart over the bowl." She used her hands to kind of show what she meant with the egg, even though she hadn't cracked it.

She eyed Garrett.

"Make sure you tap it *gently*," she emphasized that word, "on the counter to crack it. Okay?"

"I can do it. I can do it. That's easy," Garrett said, his pudgy little hand held out for the egg.

"Remember. *Gentle*." She handed him the egg.

He took it in his hand, and she helped him adjust the egg so that he didn't crack on the narrow end but around the thick middle.

"Gentle," she reminded him one last time.

His first crack was so gentle it didn't even crack the egg.

He had listened. Good.

"I think you can do it a little bit harder. Just a little."

The pinched look of concentration on Garrett's face was adorable, and she wished she had her phone so she could take a picture. He was so cute sitting only in his pull-up on the counter, the egg in his hand, and every molecule of his body focusing on cracking the egg.

The second crack was too hard.

The egg split, and all the insides fell out, dripping down the door of the cupboard, sliding to the bottom, and plopping onto the floor.

"That might have been a bit too hard." She looked at the puddle on the floor. "But somehow you did it without breaking the yolk. That took talent."

There was a snort behind her, but she didn't turn around to look at West. This was her mess to clean up.

"We need a dog," she said to no one in particular.

"I think that is one thing we definitely don't need." West's voice held humor. "All I see is just that much more mess to clean up."

"A dog would lick this off the floor, and that would be a help right now." She put a hand on Garrett's leg. "Don't move. I don't want you to fall off."

She grabbed a paper towel and another bag and cleaned the egg off the floor.

This time when she handed the egg to Garrett, he cracked a little less hard, and she was able to help him get his thumbs in and pull the egg apart.

"Great job, kiddo." He grinned at her praise. "I don't see any shells in it. You can go ahead and take that bowl and pour it into this one." She helped him pour his egg in with the egg and milk that Warren had already added.

Things went well from there, and they had the pancakes mixed up and on the griddle in no time.

After she'd done two or three pancakes, Warren had figured it out, and she kept an eye on him standing proud beside the stove, spatula in hand, watching for the bubbles to pop so he could flip it, while she helped Garrett set the table, carrying Trevor on her hip.

West had taken Gabriella back from Hazel, and Hazel did the silverware while Garrett did the plates and cups.

"Make sure they're straight. The plates and silverware are functional, but we also want them to look pretty. It's nicer to sit at a pretty table than it is at one that's just slapped together."

Hazel nodded solemnly, but Garrett looked like he didn't have a clue of what she was saying. She assumed that must be the male-female difference and kind of grinned to herself. Even if he didn't understand, it didn't hurt him to learn.

She felt a tug at her elbow and turned to see West, looking down at her, serious.

"I'd like to talk to you later."

"Of course."

His expression held no smile, which for West wasn't exactly a shock, but he looked so serious a wave of fear went through her. Had something happened?

By the time breakfast was over, or more accurately, according to the clock anyway, lunch, it was time to put Trevor and Garrett down for their naps.

Although she was fairly certain the weather report was wrong, she still would feel more comfortable weathering "the storm of the century" in her snug little room behind the hardware store than on the road somewhere between here and there.

West held Gabriella and was feeding her a bottle when Poppy came back from putting the boys down for their naps.

Warren and Hazel were in the room, and it looked to Poppy like Warren was trying his hardest to convince Hazel to play some kind of truck game with him. She silently wished him good luck, and in her heart, she hoped that Hazel gave in.

West stood in the doorway to the kitchen, the baby in his hand, holding the bottle with his other, and honestly, her heart stopped and jumped into her throat as she saw him there.

How could a man who looked so intimidating, so strong, so unapproachable and tenebrous, look the exact opposite with a baby in his arms?

He wasn't smiling. She would term his expression more of a glower. Even that wasn't intimidating.

He looked good.

And she had a name for the feeling that buzzed through her chest.

Attraction.

Seeing him there, holding the baby, had made her long for something she had never wanted before. A family of her own.

That way lay danger.

He shifted, pushing up against the doorway, and his biceps contracted, stretching his T-shirt sleeves.

"I told you I would watch the children so you could go outside." Her eyes tore away from his and looked out the window, where the rain had been pouring down all morning. At least, she hadn't noticed if it stopped or slowed at all. She couldn't recall the last time it had rained that hard for that long. "If you'd like to go out now, I can take the baby."

"I said I wanted to talk to you." His gaze dropped just for a fraction of a second, and it made her feel like he wasn't as confident as he looked. "Is now a good time?"

"Why don't you go outside and do what you need to do, and if you still have something to say to me, you can do it when you come in. In the meantime, I might not stay for supper, but I'll make sure that you have something to eat and feed the children."

He nodded. "I was gonna suggest you go. It's not snowing, but they're calling for it."

"I think I'm good until this evening. I heard it wouldn't change over until after dark."

He nodded. "I just don't want you to end up stuck here."

Right. He could barely stand her. "Having me stuck with you would be about the worst thing that could ever happen." She tilted her head and called up a cute grin. "Maybe not quite as bad as all of a sudden having four small children you need to care for."

His face lightened, although he didn't smile. "Or having an entire roll of toilet paper unrolled and stuffed into the toilet. Or cleaning poop off six pairs of underwear, or staying up the entire night with the baby who wants to do nothing but sleep during the day." He lifted a shoulder. "Two weeks ago, that might have seemed bad, but now, being stuck with you... I think I might enjoy it."

She couldn't give him a sassy look now. Not with her brows shooting up to her forehead.

She knew what he was saying, but also his tone said something else, something nicer, something she wanted to hear, but she tried hard not to take the meaning that she wanted instead of the meaning that he meant.

"I guess I'll take the baby." She started forward and held her arms out, willing herself to act the way she always had around West and to ignore the crazy things she was thinking and feeling.

It seemed impossible but also seemed extremely dangerous for him to find out what she had just recently discovered.

She was attracted to him.

Chapter Fourteen

est put the last fifty-pound sack of feed on the pile and slapped it to flatten it out.

His back hurt, his shoulders ached, and he had the bone-deep weariness that a person got after doing manual labor all day.

He loved that feeling. The feeling like he'd accomplished something that day. The feeling like he'd worked and used his body for good. The feeling like there was a place to put his supper, because he'd worked off his dinner.

He grinned because there was actually going to be a supper. One that he wasn't going to have to cook.

He looked around, and Warren was still playing in the last of the spring wheat. The little bit that was left in the grain bin.

He remembered as a kid loving to sit in the grain bin and run that soft, silky wheat through his fingers. Even more fun was to bring his toy trucks out and load them up and haul the grain around. He and his brothers had spent hours in the grain bin doing that.

They got in trouble more than once for spreading the wheat around the barn floor. They finally figured out they needed to clean up after themselves if they wanted to do it, and he'd been embarrassingly too old to play with trucks before they finally stopped.

That had been on his grandparents' farm, and maybe he hadn't stopped because he'd gotten too old. He'd stopped because they'd sold the farm.

The farming had never left his blood, and even though he figured he'd probably never be rich, knew it for a fact actually, he couldn't imagine doing anything else.

He'd never actually thought of doing it with someone.

Not until today.

Kinda crazy the way that thought had snuck up on him, slipped right through any defenses he might have put up, and settled with a sweet rightness down in his soul. Deep and good and just exactly what he wanted but hadn't known.

The rain, which had been steady all afternoon, with bursts of heavier downpours, continued to pound on the metal barn roof. It echoed through the interior and made a sound that was at once relaxing and fun to work to. It made being alone with his thoughts pleasant.

He probably spent more time than he should have, but every time he thought he'd pack up and go back to the house, he'd see something else that needed to be done, something he'd neglected in the last two weeks.

He'd left his phone inside the house, and he wasn't wearing a watch. But he knew he'd overstayed. Definitely the boys were probably up from their naps, and Poppy would be itching to leave.

He didn't want to take advantage of her. Not really. He did, however, want to talk to her. He supposed he wasn't going to get to it today since the boys were probably hungry and waiting impatiently on supper.

Maybe he could call her later.

The things he wanted to say, though, were really things he shouldn't say over the phone.

They were the things a man said to a woman face-to-face.

He didn't plan on declaring his undying love, exactly, but he wanted to say a few nice things to her. Wanted to see if they could lay a foundation for something a little deeper. Which was crazy, because it hadn't been that long ago that he wouldn't even have said that he liked her all that much.

Funny how the feelings he thought he felt weren't what he was actually feeling.

He'd been told that men could be oblivious that way.

He hadn't needed to experience it quite so dramatically in order to believe it.

What about your past?

Funny how his feelings could overrule his common sense.

He'd forgotten all about that.

Kinda crazy how Poppy could put things that he thought were so important clear out of his mind and make them insignificant next to how she made him feel.

Maybe, with a woman like Poppy, there might be a future for him.

Even a family.

He looked over at Warren, completely engrossed in the wheat, shifting it into a pile and making a road between piles.

Next time they came out, he was going to have to bring a truck or two out.

"Hey, bud, ready to go?" he asked over the pounding on the roof. Another cloudburst was coming down. Maybe they'd just mosey to the door and hope it lightened up a little before they had to walk to the house.

Run to the house.

"Can we take some of this into the house to play with? This is fun," Warren said, moving his body a little but not taking his hands out of the wheat.

"No. It'll make a mess in the house because it will go everywhere. We'll come back out to play. Maybe we can pick out some toys that would stay out here that you can play with."

"Really?"

He grinned at the surprised jubilation on Warren's face.

"Really. I used to do that when I was a kid. I know it's a lot of fun."

"You did this?"

"Sure. I played in the wheat. That's what that is. Wheat."

"Wheat?" Warren stood and looked down at his feet.

"Sure is. It's what flour is made out of. We use flour to make bread and cake and cookies and other stuff. You used it for your pancakes this morning."

"We could take some of this and make pancakes out of it?" Warren bent over and scooped some wheat up, letting it sift through his fingers and fall back to the grain bin.

"Well, technically yeah, we could, but we need something to grind it with. And normally we send it away, they grind it, sift it, bleach it..." He didn't add any commentary onto that. He didn't want to overwhelm Warren with the idea that they pretty much took everything that was good in the wheat out and then put a bunch of artificial stuff back in it and called it flour. Another day. "And then we buy the flour in the store."

"But we wouldn't have to go to the store then. You have eggs. We have wheat. We don't need anything at the store."

"Toys."

"Oh yeah. We need to go to the store for toys. And probably Gabby will need a doll. Although, I think we could make a doll too."

"Do you have something against stores?" West laughed. The kid was awful young to be taking a stand against stores like that.

Warren tilted his head and kinda looked at West like he'd never thought of that. "It's just a long ride. I hate long rides. They're boring."

"Oh." He remembered feeling the exact same way as a little kid. Funny the things one forgot when one became an adult.

"Do you think Miss Poppy will go to the store and you can watch us here so we don't have to go?"

West could only hope. It wasn't like he enjoyed grocery shopping to begin with. Add in four small children, and it became a torture session. Seriously, he'd rather walk over hot coals. Barefoot and backwards.

"I don't know."

"When Mommy feels better, she'll go for groceries. And you can watch us like Daddy used to."

Oh, boy. He couldn't even touch that. Couldn't touch that the little boy had lost his dad, not that long ago. Obviously, he still had memories of him.

And his mommy wasn't getting better.

"I'll definitely watch you so you don't have to go get groceries," he finally said, because he couldn't think of anything else. "How do you feel about walking through the rain?" he asked, knowing that would have elicited excitement out of him when he was that age.

Sure enough, Warren jumped up and threw his hands in the air. "Really? I really get to walk in the rain?" He looked expectantly at West.

West nodded. "You sure do. We have to get to the house somehow. That's where supper is. And I'm not about to let a little rain get between me and my food."

Warren nodded once, decisively putting his chin down on his chest. "Me either."

"Then let's go."

West opened the barn door and allowed Warren to squeeze through before he slipped through himself, closing the door behind him.

For some reason, Poppy's comment about needing a dog struck him as the door slid shut.

Probably Warren would really enjoy playing in the wheat with the dog around. Actually, all the kids would enjoy a dog.

What was he thinking? These weren't his kids. They weren't staying. He wouldn't allow it. And he definitely wasn't going to get a dog. It was just more work.

But the kids would really love it.

He rolled his eyes at himself as he turned, intending to start walking through the yard. But something caught his eye. Something that didn't look quite right.

It took a couple of seconds for his brain to process, and in the meantime, he put a hand on Warren's shoulder to keep him from stepping out from under the barn eave and into the rain.

The river was up. It roared with a ferociousness he'd never heard from it before. And from where he stood, although the daylight was fading, he could see that angry, brown water covered the bridge, flowing over the rickety boards.

On his list of things to do over the winter had been to pull up those old boards and put new ones over the steel beams.

Someone had used an old trailer chassis to make the bridge. The metal beams were probably still good.

He had intended to check it out and make sure.

Too late now. He just hoped it held. Regardless, Poppy wasn't going anywhere today.

That thought should have filled him with dismay.

It didn't.

He actually felt a tingle of excitement zipping through his chest and up the back of his neck.

He definitely wouldn't mind spending the evening sparring with Pollyanna.

Warren pushed closer to his side. They stood right at the edge of the overhang, and they weren't getting wet, but he thought maybe Warren was afraid of the roar of the river.

Typically, West loved the sound of flowing water. It was calming and peaceful, and it filled the country air without being obnoxious.

But the river had become a scary thing, roaring and tossing, muddy and fierce.

Loud. Fearsome. But fascinating too.

His eyes were drawn back to the house as the door opened, and

Poppy appeared in the doorway, Trevor on her hip and Gabriella in her other arm.

Hazel and Garrett stood behind her.

In his new, enlightened state, West noted subconsciously that Garrett had clothes on.

Poppy didn't look toward the river; her gaze was directed toward the barn, and he could tell when she saw him, because she jerked her head up, acknowledging him. Then she did a kind of come-hither motion with it, like she was telling him to come in.

He deduced that maybe supper was ready.

Had he really been out that long?

Daylight was fading. He certainly hadn't intended to be out so late, but time had flown by as he did job after job that had been waiting for days or even weeks to be completed.

Honestly, he felt bad. She probably had things she wanted to do.

He lifted his hand in acknowledgment and was getting ready to grab Warren's hand so they could dash through the yard to the house, staying as dry as possible, when her head turned, and he could see, even from that distance, that her eyes widened.

It wasn't hard to determine when she noticed the bridge. Her mouth opened, her jaw dropped, and he suspected if she hadn't been holding the baby, her hand would have gone over her heart.

She didn't look very happy.

He glanced down at Warren. "Give me your hand. We'll jog through the yard. I know it's fun to play in the rain, but I don't think Miss Poppy wants us walking into the house any more wet and muddy than we need to be."

Warren looked up at him with bright eyes, eager to head out in the rain.

Every kid should get to play in the rain. If he were around Warren for any length of time, he would have to make sure he got to.

"Let's go!" he called before he started jogging, slowly at first to make sure Warren was keeping up.

In a few seconds, they were on the porch, under the roof and in front of Poppy, who looked as serious as he'd ever seen her.

"I don't think I'm going to be driving over the bridge tonight," she said, calmly and firmly. Like she was afraid that he was going to make her leave.

"I wouldn't let you." The words came out before he thought about them, and her eyes flashed.

They were the wrong words.

"I don't need your permission."

"I know." But like he couldn't help himself, he said, "But I still wouldn't let you. I couldn't allow you to drive through that. The idea that I would is ludicrous."

They were the wrong words again, but maybe they were said the right way because her eyes softened, and her face relaxed.

"Be careful. I'm going to start to think you care about me."

Her expression was unreadable. He had no idea what she was thinking.

He just stared at her, not wanting to open his mouth and let the words in his heart come out.

She glanced at Warren. "Supper's ready. I was going to leave and let you eat with the kids, but I guess that plan isn't going to work. I'm going to crash at your house tonight."

She gave him another look he wasn't sure about before lifting a brow and turning around, leaving the door open as she walked away.

He wanted to laugh. Goodness, he wanted to laugh. When was the last time he wanted to laugh so badly? Or so much?

He had a feeling he was really going to enjoy spending the evening with Poppy.

Chapter Fifteen

Poppy set the cheeseburger soup on the table beside the fresh baked loaf of bread.

Hazel and she had spent the afternoon in the kitchen when they weren't taking care of Gabriella.

Race and Penny had called and said that Minnie's doctor appointment hadn't gone any better than expected and that they were going to keep her in town because of the weather.

Poppy had an idea then that she might be staying, but she'd had bread that needed kneading, Gabriella was crying and Garrett had just said he had to use the potty.

She'd kind of forgotten all about the weather then, until she'd gone outside to look for West.

Garrett set the table while Warren and West washed their hands.

That shiver of excitement that happened every time West was around was speeding down her spine right now.

It was annoying.

She didn't want to care about where he was or what he was doing, but she couldn't seem to keep from noticing.

Using a tea towel to hold the hot loaf of bread, she tried to focus on slicing the loaf and not paying attention when he walked in the room, hesitated, and then said, "That smells amazing. I didn't realize how hungry I was. And I'm sorry. I didn't realize how late it was either."

"It's okay," she said without looking up. "I kinda figured you got out there and saw all the stuff that hadn't been getting done, and time probably slipped away from you. I've done that."

"That's exactly what happened. I should have realized it was going to, at least taken something out so I could tell what time it was."

"It's really not that big of a deal, except we're stuck here tonight. I hope you don't mind."

It didn't really matter whether he minded or not, but he definitely didn't.

"Of course, I don't mind. You're the one that's been inconvenienced. And I'm sorry about that."

"You don't have to apologize again." She straightened and grudgingly allowed her eyes to fall on him as he walked around the table and sat down at the head, with Trevor in his high chair on his left. "I hadn't had a chance to talk to you about it, and maybe we can chat later, but the church was going to pay me to come out here anyway."

His brows twitched, like he hadn't realized, but almost immediately comprehension dawned on his face. "That sounds exactly like something that my parents would do. Not just for me, for anybody."

"That's right. We didn't really hash out the details, but the point was that you needed help with the kids."

West nodded, but if he had feelings about it, they didn't show on his face.

Although he seemed lighter somehow, probably because of getting some of his work done, his familiar scowl was back on his face. He did grin as Trevor beat his little child-sized fork on his tray and said something that sounded an awful lot like, "eat, eat, eat."

"Hold on a couple minutes, buddy. We have to wait for everyone to be ready."

"I'm ready now," Poppy announced, with a grin at Trevor, trying to keep the dismay off her face as she looked around the table.

The only seat left was the one right in front of her. The one to the right of West.

It wasn't exactly what she planned, but she wasn't going to be rude or make a big deal about moving her plate and chair and sitting somewhere else.

West prayed and they passed the food, with West helping Trevor and Poppy making sure Warren and Garrett were situated.

"You were out of vegetables, or there would be some green on the table right now." Poppy put the ladle back in the pot of cheeseburger soup and picked up her spoon.

"What can I say? Vegetables are the most exciting thing in the grocery store, and when I bring them home, I eat them right away." West's mouth didn't even twitch. He put a spoonful of soup in his mouth and chewed like he hadn't said something so totally outrageous that Poppy wanted to sputter soup out of her mouth.

"Really? You're telling me you actually did have vegetables in this house, but you ate them all?"

"Yep."

"Even the ones in the freezer?"

"Those too."

"The children need vegetables," she finally said, not sure how to present any evidence that he didn't actually have vegetables in the house, ever, and he hadn't actually eaten them all. There hadn't been a single orange or green thing in his refrigerator, pantry, or freezer.

She was pretty sure it had been years since such a color existed inside these walls.

"Well, next time you go grocery shopping, you get whatever you want to, bring it back, and cook it, and we'll eat it." He looked around the table at the children. "Won't we, boys?"

"I don't like peas," Warren said.

"Me no like peas."

"Maybe you just never had them cooked correctly," Poppy suggested, wiggling her brows at the boys, but that didn't alleviate their scowls.

"I like potatoes. Those are vegetables. Mashed potatoes are particularly good." West gave the boys a conspiratorial grin.

"Potatoes are not a vegetable. They're..." Poppy couldn't remember what they were called, so she decided, since West was being irrational, she could be too. "They're roots. And you shouldn't be teaching these boys things that aren't true."

"I think I'm going to have to challenge you on that one. Pretty sure they are."

"Challenge accepted. You prove it."

"I have to prove it? If you're challenging my statement, you should be the one to prove that they're not."

Poppy sighed. Maybe it would be best to change the subject. The man could be infuriating.

"Garrett was dry and clean all day." She gave Garrett a thumbs-up over the table, and his little face beamed. "And he had clothes on all day too." Garrett nodded solemnly, his smile never slipping.

"Wow." West truly did look impressed. "How did you do that?"

"I promised him you'd play hide-and-seek with him tonight if he was dry and clean all day."

"Oh really?"

Poppy definitely considered that a score, because West's lips totally turned up. He even grunted. A noise that sounded suspiciously like a chuckle.

"I guess I have to congratulate you on your strategy. That was brilliant."

"I thought so. Offer a reward that someone else has to come through on." She didn't even feel the slightest twinge of guilt. "I hope you guys have fun playing hide-and-seek tonight."

"Did you tell him that you're playing too?"

"I most certainly did not. *You* are the reward. I'll probably have to be feeding the baby or something."

"I don't agree to play hide-and-seek without Poppy. We can't play unless she plays with us, can we, boys?" West looked around the table very seriously, and the boys all looked at him, eyes wide, and their heads shook in tandem with his. "Vote unanimous. You're in, or we're out."

Poppy laughed and rolled her eyes. "We'll see."

Hide-and-seek was something her family had played back when she was growing up, and she really hadn't thought that she would want to join in. Too many painful memories. But she found herself thinking that it might be okay. Especially when her eyes landed on Hazel, whose face was bright and shone with an eagerness that contrasted so deeply with the serious little girl she'd been when Poppy had first seen her.

Hazel should have the same memories Poppy did.

No, maybe not the same memories. But happy memories. Joyful memories of being in a family and having fun and feeling safe and secure and loved. The cares and worries of the world should not intrude on childhood.

Her eyes drifted to the little boys who had already lost a father and whose mother was fading away quickly.

And then they caught on West who had taken a scoop of applesauce and put it on his plate and was using a small spoon to feed it to Trevor. His little mouth opened up big and wide each time the spoon came toward him.

Poppy hadn't planned on West feeding him, but since the high chair was over on the other side of West, it made sense, and he hadn't said a word—had just gone ahead and done the obvious.

She supposed she'd been thinking she would have moved the high chair around.

She was glad she hadn't. West had surprised her. He was a little clumsy with the spoon, which wasn't exactly surprising. Obviously, he'd probably never fed a baby before Trevor and Gabriella had come into his life. Honestly, she would be clumsy with the spoon, too.

And now, shocking her, she was curious about his past. Wanted to know more about him.

It was probably because of that annoying attraction or the buzz of excitement. Whatever. She had to clamp her lips closed over questions that wanted to tumble out.

West ate fast. He was able to feed the baby and finish his food in the amount of time it took her to eat her own stuff and help the other kids.

They finished up supper, with the kids chatting about what they had done inside and Warren telling the boys what West and he had done out in the barn.

She was carrying the empty pan that had held the hamburger soup out to the kitchen when West stopped her, leaning down after looking around at the kids and saying low in her ear, "Normally after supper if Minnie doesn't come out, we go in and all the kids talk to her. Since she's not here, I suppose we should give them baths and get them cleaned up, and then we can play hide-and-seek. If you were serious about that." He lifted a brow. "I'm not doing it if you don't."

"You can be brave."

"I am brave. I'm going to play a game with you. And if I'm really brave, I might let you find me."

She laughed, still surprised that someone that she thought had been so dark could make her laugh so much. "No. No special favors. There's just no way you can actually find a place to hide where I won't find you."

"We'll see about that." He straightened and made like he was going to walk away before he stopped and leaned back down. "I really would like to talk to you after the kids go to bed. If you can make some time for me, I'd appreciate it."

She stared at him for just a second. Their eyes met. Something crackled in the air between them. Some kind of tension, or little pricks of excitement. But his face was serious, with not a hint of any of those emotions.

It was all her.

Maybe he wanted to lay out the schedule he wanted to keep with the kids. Or something they had to do with Minnie.

Or maybe some kind of proposition for cooking and cleaning.

She turned her head away. "Of course, I'll talk to you. We need to get some things figured out with the kids."

"That's..." West trailed off.

Garrett ran up to them. "I have to pee. I have to pee."

"All right. We'll do that right now," West said, with just a hint of panic in his voice, like he wasn't totally confident that even though Garrett had told him he had to pee that he could actually wait to pee.

Poppy didn't want to watch him leave. She wanted to get right back into what she was doing, but her eyes kind of hooked on him as his hand reached down, and Garrett's slipped into his, and they hurried off to the restroom.

She certainly had gotten a more rounded glimpse of West since Minnie and her kids had moved in.

Hazel stood on a chair and helped her do the dishes, and Warren emptied the dishwasher and loaded the silverware and plates back up.

It probably didn't cut down on the time that she had to spend in the kitchen, but eventually it would, for someone anyway. Whoever ended up with Minnie's children.

When West took the boys up to give them a bath, she opened the door and stuck her head out. It was too dark to see the river, but she could hear it easily, even though the rain still hadn't let up. It seemed to be much cooler out, and if she wasn't mistaken, there were some white flakes coming down with the raindrops.

If she recalled correctly, some of the weather forecasters had said there would be ice before the rain turned to snow.

She still wasn't worried about the snow lying on the ground. It never did in Arkansas. She didn't need snow. With the river up, she might not even be going home tomorrow.

Chapter Sixteen

"I want to hide by myself," Garrett said as he held West's hand while walking into the living room from the kitchen where Poppy had started counting.

Warren had already taken off after having offered to hide with Trevor, and he must have found a place because West couldn't hear any movement. To make it a little easier, they limited the places where the kids could hide to the downstairs. Still, it wouldn't take Poppy long to count to fifty, and they didn't have much time.

"Okay, buddy. Find a spot and be still and quiet."

He grinned to himself, thinking that he'd been playing pretty nice with Poppy and hadn't done any kind of trickery. They'd each been "it" about five times or so, taking turns with each of the boys and Hazel.

This was the first time he got to hide by himself. He couldn't help thinking it would be fun to scare Poppy. He was pretty sure she'd be okay with it. She was always so happy and bubbly, and he'd considered that annoying, but after being around her so much, the whole happy thing was growing on him.

Not to mention, he found he wanted to be closer to her.

Thankfully, he was wearing dark clothes, and with the clouds outside and the rain coming down, it was almost pitch black in the house.

He slipped into a corner behind his recliner but didn't hunch down, just pulled his sweatshirt up over his nose to keep his face from glowing in the dark.

"Ready or not, here I come," Poppy called from the kitchen.

Almost immediately there was giggling, but Poppy said, "Hmm. I think I hear West giggling. Only he sounds like a little boy. West, is that you?"

Garrett said, "No. It's Garrett."

"No. It *is* West. I'm giggling." West couldn't resist speaking up, knowing it would make Garrett laugh harder.

Immediately, the direction of Poppy's steps changed; they started going toward him.

"And now I think I hear Garrett in the living room. Only his voice has gotten deeper."

More giggling came from the dining room, and he heard Hazel laughing in the hall.

Funny how being around Poppy made everyone laugh. He didn't even think what she was saying was so funny. She was just being goofy, and while he could see the appeal for children, it was funny that she roped him in, too. Despite him maybe not wanting to be roped in.

Her footsteps got closer, and he tensed.

"I'm pretty sure I heard Garrett in here, although his voice sounded a lot like West's." Poppy took a step into the living room and then another. He couldn't see her face because of the lack of light, but he could see her outline. See her head swiveling, and knew she wasn't sure exactly where he was.

Which gave him the element of surprise.

She hesitated a little, and he willed himself to remain calm. He didn't want to move too soon.

The dark gave him an advantage; it also made it essential that he knew exactly where she was. He didn't want to hurt her.

But he did kind of want to scare her and also mess with her a little.

He couldn't stop his face from smiling.

He hadn't smiled this much in years. He supposed that, if anything, should tell him what kind of woman Poppy was.

The kind of woman he wanted to spend a lot more time around.

Maybe scaring her might not make her think that he was the kind of man she wanted to spend a lot more time with.

That was female logic. He shoved it aside. Scaring her would make her fall in love with him.

Wait.

Did he want her to fall in love with him?

He pushed that thought aside too.

Scaring her would make her see how strong and capable he was.

Yeah. That was definitely male thinking.

Poppy took another half-step and paused.

West shifted. A board creaked.

Poppy's head swiveled.

He moved.

She gasped, but that's all she had time for before he grabbed her, one arm around her waist, one hand clamping over her mouth.

He hadn't really intended to pull her close, but that's the way it ended up.

He pressed her to him, her back to his front, his mouth next to her ear.

"Don't scream, and I'll let the children live," he growled in her ear.

She snorted, the sound coming out her nose since he had his hand clasped over her mouth.

Her stomach shook under his hand, and it was all he could do to keep his hand from moving. She was slimmer than she looked, and she fit perfectly against him. He hadn't anticipated either one of those two things.

After her initial surprise, she rested against him, her head eventually falling onto his shoulder, with her chin partially up, and her eyes showing white in the dark as he looked down at her.

She smelled like springtime flowers, sunshine, and happiness. And there was an underlying woman scent that pulled his heart and made him forget to breathe.

He had to say something, just to prove he still could.

"Guess I better get my handcuffs out. I can tie you up and throw you in the barn for the night."

He couldn't be sure, but he thought her eyes rolled.

"Miss Poppy? Miss Poppy. Where are you?" Warren's voice came out of the dark, no fear in it, but definitely he'd noticed the silence and felt like he needed to fill it.

Poppy's arms crossed over her chest, and he thought her foot was tapping. She stared at him.

"Miss Poppy?" That from Garrett.

"Poppy, where are you?" Hazel sounded just a little concerned.

"Pop pop?" Trevor even joined in.

Under his hand, her mouth moved, probably in a grin, since it seemed like all the boys were on her side.

"I'll take my hand away from your mouth, but you need to tell the boys that I've won tonight's game of hide-and-seek."

She turned her head, and he let his hand loosen.

She whispered, "You won? How does someone win a game of hide-and-seek when they're not even 'it'? I found you. You can't win."

"Facts are irrelevant."

"Truth matters," she returned.

"I won because I captured you."

"That's not the point of hide-and-seek. The point is to not be found."

"Boys," West said in a louder voice. "I've captured Miss Poppy, and that makes me the winner for the night."

"What?!" Warren yelled before he said, "Come on, Trevor. Let's go get him. Where you at?" he yelled, coming in from the hall.

West shuffled to the side and hit the light switch with his elbow. "I'm right here, and here's my captive."

"Come on, guys, we can take him!" Poppy called, startling him because he wasn't expecting it, and twisted in his arms, wrapping her foot around his leg and pulling, getting his knee to bend.

They fell over the arm of his recliner together before sliding onto the floor. West twisted to keep Poppy from landing on her back. Through the chaos, he didn't miss the big grin on her face. It looked smug yet not in an unkind way. He supposed his own grin matched it.

The boys and even Hazel plowed on, and there was some tickling and wrestling happening as the boys mostly seemed to be jumping on him.

Poppy wiggled back, and he let her go, disappointed but not having any excuse to keep her.

He supposed he should have known with the way he'd been feeling toward her that holding her would be better than he'd expected.

He probably also should have known that he wouldn't want to let her go.

But though things had surprised him, and even while the kids were bouncing on his stomach and trying to tickle his armpits, part of his attention was on Poppy as she walked out of the room.

Then he realized the baby was crying. That was probably where she was going.

He had the kids pretty wound up, and he ended up reading them a couple of stories after he put them in their beds to calm them down.

By the time he was finished, Poppy had Gabriella fed and burped and was setting her back down in her crib.

He waited outside the room, watching as Poppy laid the baby down, smoothed her hair with gentle strokes of her fingers, and then stood for a few seconds beside the crib looking at the porcelain skin, the dark eyelashes, the rosebud mouth, and the little curled body.

He could only imagine what she was thinking. Maybe wishing for a baby of her own, although he'd never heard Poppy say anything about a family.

Maybe wondering what was going on with Gabriella's mother, feeling bad that the little one had lost both mother and father.

She turned and seemed surprised to see him standing in the doorway. Her step hesitated before her shoulders squared and her chin came up, and she walked to the door.

He stepped back to let her pass and closed the door, leaving it open a crack.

"Did you see it snowing?" he asked softly, unsure why he thought she would enjoy it but maybe just wanting to see her smile.

"No? The last time I looked out, I thought I saw a few little white things; it's snowing for real?"

Her face brightened, just like he thought it would, and she hurried to the window.

"Come on. Grab your coat, and we can go out and stand on the porch...if you have a few minutes?" He added that last after hesitating, not wanting to seem bossy, even though he was.

She walked ahead of him down the stairs and grabbed the jacket she'd worn that morning.

Funny how time flew sometimes, and yet it seemed like forever ago that she'd arrived and he hadn't even had breakfast finished.

He put his own coat on, then opened the door for her.

Big white flakes fluttered down, easily seen despite the darkness.

"Holy smokes! The ground is covered already! Maybe we'll get the snow they called for."

"They said a foot maybe."

The snow seemed to mute sounds and just soften everything, although the river still roared in the distance.

"That sounds really angry."

"Maybe we should have gone out the back door. It's probably not as loud back there."

"We can walk around."

He started out onto the step, and under his boot, he could feel the snow, squishy and also slippery.

"Give me your hand. It's slick."

There was a brief hesitation, then her hand slipped into his, feeling alive like the rest of her body.

It had been a bad idea to grab her. It would be a long time before he forgot that.

They walked down the steps, the snow crunching under their feet, and around the house.

"That did make it a little quieter."

"And it's just as beautiful back here. We hardly ever get to see snow fall in Arkansas."

"A couple of times a year usually. Seeing it lie on the ground like this is fun, too."

"I remember being so excited when I was a kid to see it snow. We should probably get the boys up and let them watch."

He loved the boys, at least he liked them a lot, but he didn't really want to get them up right now. He was enjoying this time with Poppy. He didn't want it to end.

"I think I'm worn out from watching kids for one day. And I didn't even have them all afternoon. I wanted to thank you for that."

"Not a problem." She lifted her shoulder, and then she put her hand out, laughing as the snow landed on it and watching as the big flakes melted into a puddle of water on her palm. "Most of the time, I enjoy kids. But they are a lot of work. It's easy to see you were overwhelmed."

"I was handling everything quite well, thank you."

"One of the kids was completely naked when I walked in. I don't consider that handling everything well. I'm pretty sure the rest of the world might put some qualifiers on that as well."

"Hey, he was alive, and fed...almost fed...and clean and warm. I was doing pretty good. Even if I have to praise myself."

"Let another man praise you and not your own lips?" She grinned, maybe making fun of him a little that his father was pastor.

"I wasn't always a PK. In fact, I started my life as a farmer's kid. I guess that's why I'm here now."

"Once a farmer, always a farmer?"

"I guess it doesn't hit everyone like that. But I sure got it going that way."

"This is not what I thought about you."

"Thought?" he prompted

She shook her head but didn't say anything more, and he couldn't stop himself from asking, "What did you think?"

"Don't be offended. But I think 'darkness.'" She said it kind of easily, not like she was insulting him, just like she was casually talking about the snow or about supper.

"I guess there is some in there. I'm working on it. Or maybe I should say God's working on me. Interesting that you should say that though, because when I think of you, I think 'light.'"

She laughed. "It's a deliberate cultivation on my part, because..." Her voice trailed off, and she put her hand out again, touching the snow, like she didn't want to think about what she was about to say.

He wanted to find out what she was gonna say. In fact, he thought he might outright ask her about her past. But not right now.

Chapter Seventeen

"I told you I wanted to talk to you, because I wanted to thank you. I appreciate you staying today. Appreciate you helping me before." West spoke sincerely, hoping Poppy knew he truly meant what he said.

She'd turned to him and was listening. It was harder to talk when she met his eyes, so he looked over her head.

"You're right. I don't like to admit that I was overwhelmed. I don't think that's anything any guy likes to say. You know, we like to give the illusion at least that we're in control of everything. But I needed you. And you didn't give me a hard time about it, and you could have. I haven't always been the nicest to you. So, yeah, thanks."

He took a breath when he was done, glad he managed to get it all out. He shoved his hands in his pockets, leaning his shoulder against a porch beam, looking out at the snow as it fell. It really was pretty, although not something he would normally sit around and stare at.

Somehow though, watching snow fall seemed like fun when Poppy was beside him.

"Well, I told you that the church asked me to do it. Although, I wasn't supposed to start this soon. But Miss Penny seemed to really want those pull-ups out here today."

"Obviously, I needed them."

"Not you. Unless you have something else you want to tell me?"
He chuckled.

Then he sobered. While he was saying things, he might as well tell her. "You make me laugh easier than anybody else. How do you do that?"

"When the light and the dark combined, the light always wins." Her words were gentle. She wasn't lecturing him. "I told you. I read the back of the book. I win."

Of course, she was right. He didn't think of himself as darkness, though.

"After my parents died, I went to a foster family. That's where I met Minnie. She was there too. There wasn't a whole lot of supervision, and there were some really awful things that went on in that house. But it was the friends I fell in with and the things I did with them that really took me down. They were into a lot of séances and devil worship, black was a good color. Just dark stuff. It was only a few months, but it's amazing how you can walk away from everything you've been taught when everything around you is nothing but a deep pit."

He realized he was actually pushing into the post with his shoulder, and he forced himself to relax. "I can see now how stupid I was, but it kind of marks you. If you give the devil a hold, he pushes the door down. It's really hard to clean house after he's been there."

She didn't say anything, and he thought maybe he scared her. Devil worship wasn't a joke; he'd been too young to know any better.

Maybe he shouldn't have told her. Wasn't something he told too many people.

"Was Minnie in that too?"

"We all were to some extent." He hated to tattle on her, but he couldn't lie to Poppy.

"So she knows about you?"

"Yeah. We never talk about it, though. There are just some things you can't talk about."

"I understand that."

"I was kinda hoping you would. Talk to me about what makes you understand. You keep alluding to it, and I'm curious."

"You're curious? About me?" she asked lightly. Like she wanted to tease him instead of be serious.

He'd let go of her hand after they'd gotten to the porch. But now he pushed off the post and walked over to where she stood in front of the banister, her hands on it, now leaning over the railing with her tongue out.

"If you're trying to get a snowflake, you'll probably have to get off the porch. You're never gonna stretch far enough to get out from underneath the eave without falling over the banister."

"Maybe I *want* to fall over the banister. Maybe that's preferable to telling you what you want to know about me."

"Hey. It can't be that bad. Can't be worse than what I've done."

What in the world could she have done? What could make her so ashamed that she couldn't admit it, especially after what he'd said?

She straightened, then turned, propping her hip on the banister and facing him. Her arms crossed over her chest, and she looked up at him.

"I suppose you'll be angry at me if I don't tell you?"

He hesitated for a minute. Time slipped by between them. He didn't want to give her an answer that wasn't true.

"I guess I just told you something that not too many people know about me. But that doesn't mean that you're required in any way to do the same. I don't want you to feel like you have to. And no. I won't be mad. It's your right to either tell me or not."

"You know, I want to trust you. And just for the last few minutes, I've been biting my tongue over trying to say anything. I've never had to do that before."

"No pressure." He truly meant that. As much as he was even

more curious now than he had been, he definitely didn't want to hurt her. "If it's going to upset you. Don't worry about it."

"It probably will. But I'm going to tell you anyway." Her voice was firm. "You might even have heard about it. Some people have. It's one of the stories that are so unbelievably bad it made the national news."

His stomach balled up. Maybe he shouldn't have pushed. He had a feeling he didn't want to hear what she was going to say.

"I grew up on a farm too. I was the third child out of eleven children. When this happened, my mom was pregnant with Hazel. She and my dad and I were doing the milking that morning." She let out a hard breath. "We all took turns. It was just my morning." She lifted a hand, as though that thought needed extra emphasis—that it was randomly her turn to milk. "That's just the way it was. It was winter, and we had a fire in the woodstove in the kitchen. I know, people don't have woodstoves anymore. But when you have eleven kids, you have more help than you do money. And wood was free. We actually heated our whole house with it. And in northern Missouri where we lived, it got a lot colder than it does here."

He got the feeling she was giving him extra details just because she was trying to build herself up to saying whatever it was that she needed to say.

He let her talk.

The real temptation was to close the distance between them and put an arm around her. It probably wouldn't make things easier for her, but it would make him feel better. He'd been wanting to do it for a while.

"Dad had fixed the fire, got it going in the woodstove. My sisters would be getting up in an hour or so to make breakfast which would be on the table when we were done milking the cows. My brothers would be getting up about the same time to come out and feed, but it didn't take quite as long to feed as it did to milk. We always had everything out and ready for morning the night before." She laughed a little. "We all liked to sleep in as long as possible. So we did as much the night before as we could. I suppose that's the way all farmers work."

He had to laugh a little at that. "I don't milk cows, but I can relate. It's almost always easier to do the work the night before than it is to get up early the next day."

"Exactly. And we already got up at four."

"Wow."

"Anyway, I guess it was a flue fire. That's what the fire inspector said anyway."

A sick feeling of premonition crawled through his middle.

"I don't know what it was that made Mom look out the door while we were milking. Usually we kept everything closed up tight to keep the warmth in. Maybe it was a mom's intuition. I don't know. Anyway, when she looked out, the house was fully engulfed."

West couldn't help it. He gasped. The statement she'd made ran through his mind. She was third of eleven.

"You had ten siblings in that house."

"I did." She put a hand out to the snow but didn't seem to watch the flakes land in it, caught up in her story. "Mom called 911. Dad ran across the path from the barn to the house. My brother Adam was one, and he and Abigail, my oldest sister, were looking out the window of his room on the second story. I can still see them in my mind right now. Looking out."

She didn't say anything for a minute. Flakes melted in her hand, and she didn't seem to notice. It had to be getting cold. West reached for it, taking it and folding it in his. She didn't resist.

"Abigail looked serene. I think she knew exactly what was going to happen. She'd probably already tried to get out and couldn't. And even though the smoke swirled around them, Adam was calm. I remembered distinctly that he wasn't crying. But he was in front of her, like she was holding him up to look out the window."

She swallowed. "There were five windows across the front of the house. I can see my other siblings in different ones. I try not to picture them though, because they were not like Abigail. Esther, she was only 15 months younger than me, and we did everything together, had a window open, and she was crying and screaming." Her hand flexed in his before tightening into a fist. "I don't need to say anything more. You understand, I'm sure. It was an awful time. I was the only sibling that survived. And my dad ran in, even though the house was consumed. I guess he thought he might be able to save someone. He ended up dying too."

The snow was still falling; the night was still dark. The river still roared in its muted way. West's heart still beat, and his lungs still filled and emptied. But it felt like the whole world had shifted.

He'd made a lot of assumptions about the woman standing in front of him.

They'd all been wrong.

"You and your mom were the only ones of your family left?"

She looked at the snow, nodding. She couldn't even look at him. "That's right."

He crossed his arms and turned, leaning against the banister with his thighs, looking up at the snowflakes falling down whimsically.

How could God let something like that happen to one family?

Then the thought struck him. "Where's your mom?"

Poppy turned beside him, and she leaned a hip against the banister again. Still, she kept her hands over her chest crossed, probably for protection.

"She and I handled things differently. We both saw everything happen, and it was months before I woke up and spent a day that I didn't cry." Her chin came up. "But one day, I got up and I decided it wasn't gonna be the way I spent the rest of my life. I'd grieved long enough. I don't mean to say that I didn't grieve. I did. And you need to. But happiness is a choice, and if the joy of the Lord is my strength, then I needed to live that, no matter what trials God gave me."

Her lips turned up, ever so slightly. "Every day since then, I've tried, some days with more success than others, to live the truth." She put her hands down on the banister, her knuckles white as she squeezed. "My mom struggles with depression. I don't think anyone could blame her for that. She can't really function outside of an institute. Thankfully, there's one near where we were, and she has a scholarship to stay there. That's how I ended up on my own."

"Hazel?"

"Hazel's personality seemed to be becoming affected by my mom's depression. And even though seeing her brings those images to my mind, the images in the window, I couldn't not take her."

"I see."

"Yeah. And now you can see why I said I was never getting married, never having children. I've already lost a family once. No person should be expected to go through that again."

All the breath seemed to leave him, although not necessarily in one fell swoop. His lungs just started deflating. The air kept going out, and he couldn't seem to pull anything in.

It wasn't what he wanted to hear, definitely.

But it also made a lot of sense. He couldn't deny that either.

"The joy of the Lord is your strength. That's good. That's Bible."

"I know."

"So you think God doesn't want you to have a family? You think he wants you to make the decision you made about never having one?"

She whirled on him, her mouth open, anger in her eyes, just that fast. But she didn't get any words out.

Slowly, he could see she was giving credence to his words. Thinking about them. Rolling them over.

"It's funny, because until a week or so ago, I said the exact same thing. I've never been interested in getting married and having children. Maybe it was the darkness I saw in the world, was a part of, that made me feel like I didn't want to bring kids into that. But I guess the little guys who are sleeping in my house right now made me feel like maybe my life has been a selfish one."

He wasn't sure whether he should add more or not. She had never given any indication that she had any kind of feelings toward him at all. But after what she told him, he felt like it was probably necessary for him to say something dangerous.

He brought his other hand up, smoothing his fingers over her knuckles before enclosing it in both of his, like protection.

"I always enjoyed our sparring. I don't even think I would have admitted it, but I always looked for you in church, and maybe walked by you, just so we could exchange barbs. It was fun. I felt like we were both goofing off, and we both knew it, and neither one of us had to worry about hurting anyone's feelings." He didn't think he was wrong about that. "But working with you the last few days, I realized that whatever that feeling was, the one where I look for you and enjoy bantering with you, had worked its way into more. And I get that you might not want a husband and family, and after suffering that loss, I can't blame you. But if there's anyone in this world that I can do that with, it would be you. I..."

He almost said it wouldn't take much for him to fall in love with her, but he had to shut that thought down.

She wasn't ready for that.

He most certainly wasn't ready for it either.

Chapter Eighteen

*W*as she actually tempted to close the distance between West and her?

It's true they'd been working well together with the children, and their bantering had become more fun than sarcastic, but that tug of attraction that she'd been fighting had become stronger and she wanted to...?

Step closer...step into his arms.

She needed to hold on to the banister to steady herself. Because yeah, she could see herself doing that.

Maybe she should say something. Something that acknowledged what he said. That maybe she was feeling the same.

But she couldn't think of something that wasn't too revealing. After all, she'd dredged up all of those old memories and spoken about them for the first time in a really long time, and maybe she was just feeling emotional.

Maybe she should be clear about where she stood.

"I guess you can understand, after everything I said, why I don't have any interest in getting married or having children. I love them.

Children that is. It is not that I don't think about getting married sometimes too. It's just…"

"You don't ever want to go through that again." His words sounded flat and almost matter-of-fact.

"That's exactly right."

"I guess I've had thoughts like that too. Because of losing my parents. Man…" He ran a hand through his hair, back and forth over his head, before dropping it again. "You don't know how that rips the rug out from underneath you. Everything you thought about your life, gone. And then, to land in a foster home like the one I did. I was angry. I needed to get away. It was easy to go over to the other side." Shoving a hand in his pocket, he looked up at the snow. No answers there, just something to focus his eyes on. "I don't want to go through that again. Not that you can lose your parents twice. But when you care for someone, when you care for a lot of someones— family, a wife, kids, you sacrifice and work for them. There's no guarantee that they're not going to walk out. There's no guarantee they're going to live. There aren't any guarantees. And it's just safer to not even go there."

"That's exactly right. And I've already been through it, why would I put myself through that again?"

He nodded, and they turned toward each other, looking at each other like they'd never seen the other one before.

She'd never met someone who understood so completely what she'd gone through. How she felt.

"Most of the time when I tell people I don't want kids, and I don't want to get married, they tell me that I'm crazy. They think I don't know what I really want, that I'll change my mind."

"They don't really understand," he said softly.

Somehow, they'd moved closer to each other. Although she couldn't say whether it was because she'd taken a step or he had.

"Right. They see me smiling, they see me happy. They see me playing with children and enjoying it. Honestly, they see my true love for kids."

"They probably look at you and see someone who would make a perfect wife and an amazing mother."

"Maybe. I guess."

"They don't understand what's happened in here." He tapped his chest.

"Right. And how scared I am to have it happen again."

He nodded, the hand that had tapped his chest reaching out and pushing her hair back, his fingers trailing through it and settling on the slope of her shoulder, his thumb tracing the line of her jaw.

"They see a beautiful woman who has a lot to offer someone. A woman who deserves to be loved, and cherished, and protected. Who doesn't deserve to go through that kind of pain again."

He was saying all the right words, but his tone had changed, containing some kind of warm undertone that made her want to close her eyes and lean into his palm.

Her hand came up and slid over his, feeling the strong cords in his wrist, the warmth of his skin, and the scratch of the hair on his arm. "You understand, because you've been through it too."

"That's right. People have said similar things about me."

"You're the most eligible bachelor in church. I've heard it. They point you out as a hard worker, dependable, and of course, you're a little dark and a little scary. For some reason, that's so attractive to women."

He lowered his head a bit, and she lifted hers.

"Is it attractive to you?"

In another man, that question might have seemed like he was fishing for a compliment or insecure. But with West, it didn't seem that way.

Rather, it felt like he was asking out of concern for her, in consideration for how she felt. Regardless, it loosened her lips and made her want to be completely honest.

"Maybe not someone else. But in you, yes. Maybe I saw the pain underneath. Because when I looked at you, I always felt like you understood. Which is a weird thing to feel, but it's true." Her fingers slid up his forearm, lightly, and she breathed deep of the scent that made her feel safe and somehow excited at the same time.

"Same. I could tease you because I knew you understood. I picked on you, because we felt like opposites, but somehow, there was always that underlying knowledge that you knew."

Somehow, his arm had slid around her waist, and she took the last step to close the distance between them.

Their breath mingled as snowflakes fell softly beside them, and the night air was still.

"I want to kiss you."

His words caused the heat that had been curling in her stomach to tighten sharply before spreading out in warm ribbons.

There was no hesitation in her answer.

"I want that too."

West didn't say any more, and she didn't need him to.

His head descended, her arms wrapped around his neck, and she pressed against him as his lips met hers.

Never in her wildest dreams would she have imagined standing on West's porch in his embrace, kissing him and feeling like her whole world had turned into something beautiful and magical and yet solid and steady and safe with his arms around her, anchoring her.

Her heart catapulted in her chest, and she wanted to be closer, to lose herself in the heat of his body and the strength of his arms and the feel of his mouth on hers.

She didn't whimper when he pulled away, but she wanted to. Which made her smile.

His grin matched hers.

"That smile is a beautiful thing," he said.

"I thought it annoyed you," she said, and there was only flirt in her voice. "Maybe your eyes are bad."

"Men aren't known for being in touch with their emotions. I think what I thought was annoyance was actually attraction."

"Oh, you are good."

West didn't exactly giggle, but they definitely chuckled together.

"Will you think I'm greedy if I tell you I want to do that again?"

"When people look at us, they see opposites. It's funny how we want the same things."

His grin widened, and it thrilled her the whole way to her toes and back.

"I like the way you think."

"You have some pretty good ideas yourself."

"Speaking of ideas, I had one I want to run by you."

"Yeah?"

His hand ran up and down her back, slowly, making her shiver.

"My mom mentioned that Minnie hadn't had a Christmas with her children." He spread his hand at the snow. "We've got the snow. We've got the kids. And we're stuck here. What do you think about getting the tree out, and the Christmas decorations I have, which are not a lot, and decorating the house for Christmas tomorrow? I'm assuming we're not going to be going anywhere."

Poppy had to admit she was shocked. "I can't believe you thought of that."

"Pretty deep. I impressed you?"

"You did."

"I can't help but notice the lady didn't say my kiss was impressive."

Poppy leaned back in his arms, looking up, half of a grin on her face. Wondering. She supposed he was probably kidding. Still.

"You know, I couldn't say you're the best kisser in the world. I couldn't even say you're the best kisser in Mistletoe. I really don't know. I've not kissed every guy in the world or even all the men in Mistletoe."

"I think I'm happy about that."

Her lips tilted. "I can say though, that's the first kiss I've ever had that made me feel hot and cold at the same time, and safe and excited, and I'm just thankful that someone didn't interrupt us and ask me to say my name, because I'm not sure I could have."

"That good?" His grin might have been a little cocky. Her honest words had pleased him.

She nodded. "But I don't think it's skill. I just think it's you."

"That's good. I don't need to have that effect on every woman in the world. In fact, I'm pretty happy not having that effect on every woman in the world or, more precisely, any *other* woman in the world. You're the only one that I care about."

"You sound a little surprised."

"Not that you're the only one. But that I care about you. It wasn't a surprise, I guess, just...fear."

"I have that same feeling. Kissing you makes it go away."

"Then I guess I have a job to do. I'd better roll up my sleeves and get started."

"You do that. I'll let you know if the second one is as good as the first."

They were on the porch for a really long time after that.

Chapter Nineteen

"I think the water has gone down far enough. I'll slip out before the kids get up from their naps and check and make sure the boards are good."

West held the cell phone to his ear and looked out the window at his driveway. The bridge seemed like it had weathered the flood no worse for the wear. The kids had had a great time playing in the snow all morning. They'd been completely worn out and could barely keep their eyes open over lunch.

While he'd been out playing with Warren and Garrett, Poppy had gone through his Christmas decorations and gathered a few odds and ends. She'd also rooted through his house, found some things she could use, and made some more.

They were planning on getting his artificial tree out while the children slept and then decorating it this evening.

He'd called his dad to tell him about their plans, and Race was now taking it even further.

"Hospice is ready to come out, and Minnie is eager to get back to the children. She is sleeping right now though, and after her online appointment doctors are trying to make sure that the pain is managed. It's getting worse."

"I think we're doing this just in time."

"I think you're right. Penny will spend the afternoon gathering up gifts and getting them wrapped, and we'll see if we can do this as a surprise. I might even be able to get us a Santa Claus and possibly an elf."

"The kids would love that."

"That's what I thought. You text me with anything else you need, and we'll see what we can do. I don't want the church to descend on her too hard—she can't handle it. I'd even like to keep hospice staying back if we can and just let it be Minnie and her children, with you and Poppy."

At this point, Race hesitated. It seemed like he wanted to say more but stopped himself just in time.

Race cleared his throat. "I believe Minnie wants to talk to you about the kids."

"Is she not happy with what we're doing with them?"

"It's not that. Probably the opposite."

"She's okay with Poppy?"

"Of course. There's not a better woman anywhere to be taking care of children. Poppy's good with kids, and she has never-ending patience." His dad snorted. "She's got more patience than I do."

"I suppose she could give your sermon on Sunday if you want her to."

"Very funny, son."

"You know, Dad, I don't think I've ever said anything to you for what you've done for me. I don't thank you often enough. What you did for my siblings and me...the things I put you through...you didn't give up on me. I appreciate that. I'd be a much different person today if it hadn't been for you and Mom."

"Thank the Lord. He's the one who worked it out. I never thought I'd be a dad."

"You made a good one."

"You will too."

This is where West would have argued with anyone else.

Yesterday.

Today, with the memory of Poppy's lips under his, and her body pressed close, and her smile that warmed him the whole way to his soul, and her whispered words that he was the only one—yeah, he could see himself being a dad. As long as Poppy was the mom.

Funny how his brain had shifted that fast and that completely.

But he had never been the kind of person to wallow around in indecisiveness.

"Think you might be right, Dad. They're going to have a great set of grandparents."

His dad chuckled. "I owe your mom a pizza."

"What?" How had his dad changed the subject so completely and so fast? What had he missed? Pizza? "Are you bringing pizza for the Christmas celebration?"

Laughter came through the phone again. "No. It's a personal thing. Your mom's already taking care of the food. It'll be coming too. She's got everything lined up. She was born to do this job."

"As were you."

"I think you're right about that. When God calls us to do something, we're fools if we hesitate. But sometimes, it takes a lot of faith to just step out when there's no floor underneath your foot."

West rubbed his eyes, looking at the tracks that the kids made through the snow, trying to figure out what his dad was saying.

Sure, he was talking about his own walk, but it was almost like he was saying something more. Some lesson he wanted West to grasp, but it just wasn't coming to him.

"I'll take your word for that, Dad. You're the wisest man I know."

"Just follow Jesus, son."

They hung up not long after, and West ran out, checking the boards on the bridge. They seemed remarkably none the worse for the wear. He could hardly believe it.

Deep in thought, he returned to the house. Walking in, he looked around. Poppy came down the stairs, and she didn't have a baby in her arms.

"Are they all sleeping?"

"Even Warren. You have exhausted those poor children." That smile, the one that never stopped, graced her lips. "Although, I think you were playing just as hard as the children. Maybe you should take a nap too."

He shook his head. "No way. I'm not taking a nap or doing anything that would make me miss any time with you."

He wouldn't have thought her smile could get any bigger, but it did, and he loved it.

"My parents have everything arranged, and they're expecting to bring Minnie tomorrow. Hospice will be hot on their heels though, and Dad doesn't think we have much time with Minnie."

"That doesn't surprise me." She stopped in front of him. "It does make me sad though. All those little babies upstairs, no parents."

They stared at each other for a minute, her smile not quite as bright as it had been, of course. The whole thing was sad.

It didn't keep him from wanting to kiss her though. Still, along with the urge to put his arms around her, came an idea. One so crazy and outlandish, and to be frank, before last night, one he would never have given the light of day to.

"What?" she asked, tilting her head. "What are you thinking?"

He needed some time to think about it. He wasn't sure how he felt about it, and he didn't want her to get on the bandwagon before he was ready; it would hurt her if he didn't go along with it.

"I'm thinking the same thing I thought last night. I'd rather kiss you than do anything else."

"But I have no idea why you're standing there looking at me."

He was slow to answer, just because her words hit him hard just the right way.

"I'm thinking, if I don't take you in hand, you might end up being kinda bossy."

He slid his arms around her waist and pulled her toward him, wrapping his other hand around the nape of her neck and holding it while she turned her head up, a smug grin settled on her face.

"Take me in hand? Really? What is this, like 1980?"

He snorted out a laugh. "1980 isn't that long ago."

"Maybe to an old dog like yourself. To a young chick like me, 1980 is ancient, back when men were Neanderthals and took their women 'in hand.'" She mimicked his voice as she quoted his words and gave him a challenging look.

"I think, when a woman talks like that, what she really means to say is, 'West, I want you to kiss me.'" He ran a thumb over her cheekbone. "You need to learn to say what you mean."

"West, kiss me."

THE HOUSE SPARKLED. The Christmas tree sat in the corner, decorated with the lights that Poppy had found in his basement along with bulbs, strings of popcorn she and the kids had made, paper circles, and she'd even baked some kind of thing that kind of looked like cookies that she and the kids had decorated with paint last night.

They'd been full of energy after their long afternoon naps.

It wasn't the most beautiful tree in the world.

Far from it. But it looked like a tree that had lots of love on it.

He almost snorted at himself. Being around Poppy had completely changed even the way he thought.

It changed him.

"You've got that look on your face again," she said.

A crash came from the living room, and both of them stared at each other, waiting.

A scream. But not a life-or-death scream.

"Sounds like Garrett ran his truck into the wall."

"Sounds like Garrett made out better than the wall did," Poppy said with a raised brow.

"I guess we'll fix that. Tomorrow."

She lifted both brows, and when he didn't respond, she said again, "That look? Explain."

He'd been teasing her, and his teeth showed. "I don't want you to get a big head, but I was thinking about how you've changed me. Or, I should say, how I've changed because of being around you."

"Changes?" She lowered her head a little, and he read that look easily.

"Good changes. All of them. It's a true blessing when you can see that the person that you're with has influenced you to make changes that have made you a better person."

"Then that's a good thing."

"Yeah."

"And here I thought you were excited about Santa Claus coming."

"Shhh! You don't want the kids to hear that. That's supposed to be a surprise."

"Well, it probably really will be a surprise. Usually Crew and Burgundy do it, but Penny texted me and said at first that there wasn't going to be a Santa Claus, and then she texted later that they'd found substitutes."

"Really? Who?"

Poppy shrugged. "I'm not sure."

Gabriella stretched, and they both looked down at her.

Her little mouth opened in a big yawn. Her eyes scrunched up, then her mouth closed and the corners of her lips turned up, and they both hooted at the same time.

"Oh my goodness! She smiled!" Poppy said.

"That's because she heard my voice."

"No, that scares her."

"Like it scares you."

"That's right. Scares me right into your arms."

He put an arm around her and tucked her into his side, looking out the window in time to see his parents' car coming across the bridge.

"Here comes Minnie. I'll get the kids."

He dropped a kiss on her forehead and strode into the room, gathering the boys up and bringing them out, Trevor in one arm and holding onto Garrett's hand with Warren walking beside.

He set his jaw as he saw his dad opening Minnie's door and, after she stood, picking her up in his arms and carrying her up the shoveled walk.

The snow was melting, although the ground was still covered, and the children had been out earlier that day playing in it once more.

By the end of the day, it would be gone, but it wasn't the snow that was keeping Minnie from walking.

She was probably just that weak.

Penny opened the door, and Minnie noticed right away that everyone was standing and waiting on her.

"What a welcoming committee I have. All of these handsome boys." Her smile was tremulous, and he doubted that anyone ever looked happier as her eyes swept lovingly, like a caress, over each little towheaded child standing and staring at her.

"Go ahead, Warren," West prompted.

"We have a surprise for you, Mom!"

"A surprise?" Minnie's eyes went from her boys to West then Poppy then back to West again. "What surprise?" she asked Warren.

"You have to follow me. Or Mr. Race has to follow me?" Warren said a little uncertainly.

"No. I can walk."

At her words, Race set her down, keeping his arm around her as she leaned into him. Penny came around her other side and slipped a hand around her waist.

"It's in the living room," Warren said, his eyes worried, his lip caught between his teeth.

"I'm coming. I can't wait. What could my surprise possibly be?"

Poppy had slipped away, holding Hazel's hand, getting ready to film Minnie as she walked in. West waited for them to go by before following them, the little boy in his arm hugging him close. Garrett had never let go of his hand, and he walked quietly alongside West.

Minnie got to the doorway of the living room and froze. "Oh my," she said, her hand going to her chest. "It's Christmas?" she asked, wonder in her voice. She turned, looking at West, then back to Warren, standing by the Christmas tree with a big grin on his face.

"It is! It's Christmas! And we wanted you to have Christmas with Gabriella, since she was born after Christmas."

West's eyes pricked. He blinked quickly.

Warren didn't know that they were doing it because they didn't expect Minnie to make it to next Christmas. He'd repeated what they'd told him word for word.

Somehow, it made West's breath catch and his lungs work hard to suck in more air.

Warren's innocence and his excitement for his mom to have a good Christmas with her baby pulled at West's heart.

It was sweet beyond words. West looked over, wanting to see how Poppy was doing.

Their gazes met. She was having the same problem. Blinking the liquid away. Hurting for the little boy who just wanted to make his mom happy.

"It's beautiful." Minnie stepped forward, her hand falling away from Race's arm as she walked toward her son, holding her hand out. He took it, looking so much older than his five years, and they examined the tree together.

"It looks like you might have made some of these?"

"We did! Miss Poppy made them with us. These."

He pointed to the ornaments that they'd used cookie cutters to cut out and baked in the oven on a low temperature before they used metallic paint that West had found in his garage. The flecks of metal in the paint shone and caught the light.

He'd been skeptical but had followed Poppy's lead. It had worked out a lot better than what he'd thought. The kids had a great time.

"I can see you must have painted them yourself," Minnie said, holding up Warren's hand and turning it, showing the paint that was still on Warren's fingers.

"Mr. West said it will come off before I got married. I think it looks cool."

"I do too."

The doorbell rang, and Race shifted before he said, "Warren, I think you and Garrett need to go get the door."

"Really?" Warren said, puzzlement wrinkling his forehead.

"Really. I think you might know that dude."

West moved to Poppy and put his arm around her, and she leaned into him, letting Hazel go with the boys. When he'd had this idea, he hadn't realized how bittersweet it would be. He'd thought of Christmas and Santa and presents and kids and that there'd be a lot of laughter and a lot of fun.

He hadn't expected to have his heart torn into pieces over the innocence of the children and what they were losing.

"Don't think about that," Poppy whispered to him. "Think about the beauty. And the joy. And the memories they are going to have."

"Okay, Pollyanna." He bent down to her ear, whispering before he kissed the top of her head.

"Ho ho ho, Merry Christmas!" Santa said as he walked in, carrying an armload of gifts.

Warren's and Garrett's eyes were as big as dinner plates, Hazel's matched them and even Trevor bounced in West's arm.

"Merry Christmas, everyone!"

West recognized his sister Blakely dressed in an elf uniform, complete with a hat and big ears, and carrying her own armful of gifts.

He assumed that Santa must be her best friend Martin. It seemed like Blakely and Martin did everything together.

He was sure of it when he noticed Blakely's elbow poking Santa in the ribs as she walked by him.

"Ouch," Santa said under his breath. Then, louder, he said, "You boys must be Warren and Garrett. And I think your brother Trevor is supposed to be around here somewhere."

Warren's and Garrett's heads nodded up and down, but their mouths didn't close.

"Are you really Santa?" Warren said.

"I sure am," Santa said. "Let me guess. You're Warren."

Warren gasped. "How did you know?"

"Maybe my elf told me," he said, then winked. "Just kidding. Santa knows everything, right?"

Santa talked to the kids a bit more, then they all went into the room and sat down while people from church arrived and carried casserole dishes and a roaster pan with what smelled like a ham in it into the kitchen. Race and Penny directed that discreetly, and the kids never even noticed.

West was excited about the food, but as he watched as the children chatted with Santa, and Santa talked to Minnie, and Minnie beamed over it all as she held Gabriella in her arms, and Poppy snapped pictures, and all the children gathered around Minnie, with Santa standing behind them, his arms outstretched, including them all, and Blakely, with a goofy grin and a silly elf pose, stood there too, West felt his heart thumping hard and his blood flowing lethargic, like syrup in his veins.

By the time the kids were done opening their gifts, Minnie was dragging, but she still managed to come out to the table and eat with her family, insisting that Race and Penny and Santa and Blakely stay. And even the hospice workers, after they had set up the hospital bed in the room facing the Christmas tree, were invited to sit down as well.

It was a lot of people at the table, and they ended up using chairs and stools from the kitchen in order to seat everyone, but there was plenty to go around, and everyone got full.

Despite the sadness in his heart, it was a happy day, but West couldn't get over the idea that maybe there was something more he could do.

Chapter Twenty

$\mathcal{P}$oppy tiptoed down the stairs after putting the children to bed.

She felt like she were walking with a warm glow emanating from her.

She'd never spent a nicer day.

Poking her head into the living room to check on Minnie, she was surprised to see Minnie's eyes open, watching, almost like she was waiting for her.

"Poppy. Would you mind coming in for a minute?" Minnie said, so tired her words were almost slurred together.

"I can. But just for a minute. You have to be exhausted."

"I am. And I ache all over, deep in my bones. But I didn't want to say anything while the kids were still up."

"Where's the hospice helper? Devon. Can he do something?"

"Probably. I sent him away, because I wanted to say something to you. And West."

"Devon told me to come in. He said there was that thing you wanted to talk to me about." West's voice came from the doorway that separated the living room from the dining room.

His eyes brightened when he saw Poppy, and he strode over to her, putting his arm around her but not saying anything as Minnie had started to speak.

"Thank you. I do. Something I want to say to both of you."

"Don't overdo it," West cautioned. "It was a big day."

"I know. And I wanted to thank both of you so much. I already thanked Race and Penny while you guys were putting the children to bed. And I know they had a lot to do with it. But so did you. You were the ones who decorated." She looked at the tree and lifted her hand as though to encompass everything in the room that made it look like Christmas. "And you took care of the children...Pastor Race said it was all your idea." She lifted tired eyes to West.

"It was. But I wouldn't have had the idea to do all this without Poppy. I've got a feeling all the good ideas I have from now on will be because of her."

"That's ridiculous. You've had plenty of good ideas in your life without me, and you will continue to do so."

"We can argue about that later. I'm going to win. Just saying."

"I think I'll win. But I'm definitely up to the challenge." She wanted to stare into his eyes, which was really crazy. She should have better things to do.

She did actually. So she drew her gaze away and looked back at Minnie. "I'm sorry. He's distracting."

Minnie looked serious. "From the minute you walked down the church steps the first Sunday I was here, I knew you were perfect for him. And I hadn't even seen him for years. Just from what he'd been when we'd been teenagers...he was so straight and sure, and of course, he did some things he probably wishes he hadn't—so did I—but you were a kindred spirit to him. It was so obvious when I saw you."

Her thin shoulders moved on the bed. Maybe it was a little shrug. "Since my cancer has gotten worse, it's almost like I see things that I didn't use to. Spiritual things."

That was getting a little deep, and Poppy shifted uncomfortably.

She didn't want to see anything spiritual. Not actual spirits anyway. The idea made her want to walk out of the room. Instead, she pressed closer to West, and he tightened his arm around her.

"It was in that moment, when I saw you, Poppy, on the steps, that I knew I was going to say what I'm going to say right now."

She looked between the two of them, and her fingers, which had been tracing the edge of her blanket, stilled. "I'd like for you to take my children. I want to give them to you. Whatever paperwork we need to do, it'll be easier for you and for them if we do it now. Faster. The transition'll be less bumpy. That's the thing I want, beyond what you gave me tonight, which was a Christmas with Gabriella. I know it's probably selfish of me to ask this, but I'm a mom, and my children mean everything to me. I know I'm not long for this world, and my leaving will be peaceful if I know they're taken care of. Which, if you two have them, I know they'll be taken care of."

Poppy didn't gasp, but she wanted to.

What really surprised her, though, was that beside her, West didn't even twitch. Not a move.

Had Minnie's request shocked him that much?

"Of course, that's something we'll have to think about," she began, since West seemed to be frozen in place.

"I don't have to think about it. I'll do it. As long as you're with me."

Poppy's head jerked to him. "What?"

She couldn't believe it. Yeah, sure, they'd talked yesterday some about everything changing, but...this was huge.

"I'd actually had that thought yesterday when we were talking. It was something I wanted to talk to you about, but obviously we had things we needed to do, and this is a pretty big step. But I know with all my heart it's a step I'm ready for. Only with you." His voice was confident with absolutely no hesitation.

Maybe the day had been too long, or too emotional, or there'd been too much going on, too many things to smile at, too many things to try to not think about, but Poppy was pretty sure she was going to cry.

"This is something that we should think about and pray about and take a really long time to make a decision on." She swallowed, thankful that her tears hadn't overflowed. "But I don't need to, actually. I'll do it."

"Well, I guess I should have qualified," West began, and her heart tripped. That didn't sound like cold feet, but maybe it was.

"What?" she asked, trying to make the word come out with a confident sound.

"I'll do it, but I want to marry you first."

That time, she did gasp.

"I'm sorry. I don't have a ring, I don't have a plan, and I didn't have a plan. This was not what I was thinking and not the way I wanted it to happen. But I just didn't want you thinking that this was some weird partnership that we were going to do, with the kids between us. I'm not thinking like that at all. I wanted to marry you, and I wanted to ask Minnie if she'd give us the honor of raising her children if anything were to happen to her."

His eyes moved to Minnie, and Poppy appreciated the fact that he didn't assume Minnie wasn't going to make it.

Not that anyone held any hope, but without hope, there was no point. She wanted to keep a hold of hope.

Minnie's head shook back and forth. "The honor is all mine. My children would be in better hands than they would be if I were to live. Maybe that was the Lord's doing."

"Don't say that. It's not true. You've been an excellent mom. And you've done the best you can." Poppy reached out and put her hand over top of Minnie's.

"I made a lot of mistakes. I wish I could go back and undo them."

"We've all made mistakes. All we can do is learn from them and move on. I love the way you've handled this," Poppy said. "I've not heard you complain one time."

"Isn't me getting angry at what God is giving me the same as me saying I know better than God? We all know that's not true."

Poppy's mouth snapped closed.

She probably wouldn't have said she was angry, exactly, at God. But she'd never articulated it that clearly. She resented the fire and the things that happened to her, and that was, truly, the same as her saying she knew better than God.

Guilt tightened her neck.

"That's almost exactly what I've done," West said quietly beside her. "The things that happened to me, my parents dying, what I'd done after it happened, I was definitely angry at God. And even though, maybe once Race and Penny adopted me, I did a better job of hiding it. I was still angry. And you're right. That's me saying I know better than God does."

He huffed out a breath of frustration. "How arrogant. How completely self-centered and arrogant I was that I could tell the Being that created everything I see when I look outside my window, and so much more, that I know better than He does how to run my life. It's embarrassing when I think about it now."

He looked down at the frail woman with the sunken cheeks and the dark shadows under her eyes and the bony shoulders sticking out underneath her blanket.

"Thank you. I needed that lesson tonight. I needed it for my life."

"Me too," Poppy said. "I needed it as well. I decided exactly what I could and couldn't handle after my loss, and I had decided exactly what I was going to do and wasn't going to do, and I didn't give God any say."

She turned and looked up at West.

"That was me being arrogant too."

"What did I say? We might be opposites on the surface, but underneath, we're exactly alike. Funny, neither one of us saw our arrogance and stupidity yesterday."

"No. We needed today, the Christmas, the celebration, the kids, but most of all, we needed you, Minnie. Thank you for being wise in spite of our foolishness."

Looking back, it was easy to see now how the Lord was working. If it hadn't been for the fire and the loss of her siblings, and even her mother's depression, she wouldn't have ended up where she was, with the irritating smile that caught West. And without his parents' car accident and, yeah, even the sin he got in because of it, and of course Race and Penny adopting him, they wouldn't have met. And they probably wouldn't have...fallen in love?

Maybe they really were exactly the same, because no sooner had the thought popped into her head when West said, "I guess this might be as good a time as any for me to tell you that I love you."

Normally, West's words were confident and sure, even if they were soft. But these were spoken with a touch of hesitation, and even though they both knew that the Lord had been working through it all, it was never easy to bare one's heart.

"I love you too," she said simply and easily and quickly. She didn't have to examine her heart. She'd just done it. And that's exactly what she saw.

Love for the honorable man in front of her.

Epilogue

As funerals went it wasn't terribly sad.

It could have been.

After all, four small children had just lost their mother.

But, as Blakely and Martin sat together just a couple rows from the front, they both agreed that the fact that West and Poppy had married so quickly – just a couple of weeks ago – and had gotten all the paperwork together to adopt the children – even if it hadn't gone through yet, and, most of all, that Minnie had been given the gift of one last, special Christmas with her children – and a first Christmas with Gabriella…okay, maybe it was sad.

Martin shifted as Blakely wiped her eyes.

"Here," he whispered, handing her a tissue that he'd stuffed in his pocket earlier, figuring she'd need.

They'd been inseparable since their teen years and every single wedding and every single funeral they'd attended together, Blakely had cried. Although she would deny it.

She was an accomplished horsewoman and trick rider, soon to audition for the most prestigious travelling trick riding show in America. She would never admit to the weakness of a few tears.

Being that he was her best friend, he'd let that little blip in her personality slide.

She was fun and funny and completely loyal, as well as hard-working and the only person who knew pretty much everything about him. She liked him anyway.

He could give her just as much grace.

"I never thought my brother would find happiness like this," Blakely whispered softly, around a small sniff.

"Me either." Martin leaned over to her ear. The faint scent of fresh outdoors and wildflowers came to his nose.

When had Blakely ever smelled so good?

Martin tried to focus. "I would never have paired Poppy and him together, but any fool can see they're perfect together." He meant that, too. West sat in the front pew, a little boy on his lap, and his arm around his new wife who held the baby girl.

Neither of them smiled, but there was a glow about them that indicated as clearly as a neon sign that the two of them were deeply, passionately in love.

"I have a lot of things I want to do first, but I hope I find a love like that someday," Blakely whispered, before sniffling again and quietly blowing her nose in the tissue he'd given her. Thankfully, he'd picked up several. She was as predictable as sunrise.

About some things.

Like her determination to ace the audition for the stunt riding show.

He totally supported her, even though it meant she'd be away from home for eighteen months straight. That's if the European part of the tour didn't go through. It would be three years if the show got that contract.

For Blakely's sake, he hoped it did.

He sniffed. Not because of the water in his eyes, but because he wanted to memorize the scent of the woman beside him.

He couldn't imagine being without her for three whole years. He also highly suspected Blakely hadn't thought the whole thing through, because, as much as she loved to compete, she was a homebody and wouldn't want to be gone that long.

His hands tightened in his lap as he watched Poppy's head bend over the child on West's lap. West's lips landed softly on the blonde hair in a gesture so loving, so at odds with everything he'd thought of West, that it almost gave Martin chills.

He suspected he knew someone that he could be so comfortable and so in love with.

It wasn't even a thought he could begin to entertain, so he settled down in the pew, handed Blakely another tissue and tried to focus on Pastor Race's message, which wasn't helpful. It was all about letting God have his way in your life.

Prophetic, maybe.

Join Jessie's list and be the first to know about new releases and sales on her books!

Read Dreaming of Her Best Friend's Kiss, the next book in the Cowboy Mountain Christmas series where best friends Martin and Blakely think they're outsmarting the matchmakers, but ending up matching themselves. Plus, there's a kissing contest! Keep reading for a sneak peek now.

Sneak Peek of Dreaming of Her Best Friend's Kiss

"Everyone can see the two of them are perfect together," Race Steiner said, taking a bite of the pizza.

"Everyone but themselves," his wife, Penny, gently corrected, her brows lifted in that way she had that made him want to smile and kiss her at the same time.

"You're right as usual."

Pizza wasn't their normal choice of meal with Penny being a former midwife and him a former cardiac surgeon.

Both of them knew what pizza did to the body.

However, he'd lost their bet, and that meant he owed her a pizza.

He tried to bite back a grin as he chewed on the cheesy deliciousness. He was working on getting himself into another bet. A friendly wager between a husband and wife about their children.

Only to help them, of course.

Typically, his wife won.

Which was just fine by him.

He liked pizza.

"The problem is you can't just go up and tell her that she needs to fall in love with her best friend."

"No. Definitely not." His wife tilted her head. "You've learned something over the years."

He grinned, enjoying her teasing. She knew him like no one else. "I have to give all the credit to you. At least in emotional matters of the heart anyway."

"Of course. There's nothing I can tell you about physical hearts that you don't already know."

"Emotional hearts are more complicated by far," he said with sincerity.

His wife set her pizza down, picked up her napkin, and dabbed at the sides of her mouth with a thoughtful look on her face. "It's just, everything you tell Blakely to do, she always wants to do the opposite. She's completely selfless and was always obedient and tried with a good attitude to do what we wanted, but she has this unconscious rebellion that if she knows it's what she's expected to do, she wants to do something else."

"Yeah. She's not rebellious, but it's like she hears 'can't' and sees it as a challenge."

"And hears 'can' and views it as boring."

They nodded together, their words not effective in explaining, exactly, what it was about their daughter Blakely.

Neither one of them viewed her as anything but wonderful, but she definitely always rose to the challenge, and when there wasn't a challenge, she created her own.

Penny picked up her pizza. "That's probably why she's become such a great trick rider. Most people, after they'd fallen off and broken two arms and a leg at various times, would have given up and found something slightly easier to do."

"Not Blakely. She's just as determined now as she ever was to make a living doing trick riding." Race checked the time on his watch. "Have you heard from her?" Blakely was trying out for a spot on the top traveling western show in the country.

He wished his daughter the best, and he truly did hope that she got the job, even though it was a traveling show that would take her from city to city for the next year and a half.

He hated to lose her for that long.

And he wasn't entirely sure that was the best thing for her.

But she hadn't asked for his opinion, and typically, unless there was something pressing, he tried to keep his opinion to himself until it was asked for.

Most of the time, he was successful.

"I'm sorry. I did. While you were taking a shower, she called. She's settled into her hotel room, and she's on the schedule to perform tomorrow morning at nine o'clock. I told her we'd pray for her." Penny paused with the pizza halfway to her mouth. "I didn't tell her that we would pray that she got the position." Her face was serious.

"It just doesn't sit right. Doesn't feel like that's what she's supposed to do. Did she say she's prayed about this?"

"No. I think she knows it's not really what the Lord wants for her life, but it's what she wants. And she's going after it with everything she has. Like she's always done."

Race nodded thoughtfully, his eyes on the pizza box. Part of his mind was rolling over in his head whether or not he should have another piece, and part of his mind was on his daughter, who never did things halfway but jumped in with her whole heart and soul.

It made for some really hard landings.

Lord, work this out according to your plan. Please keep her safe and close to you.

A bullet prayer. He prayed them all the time. Especially for his children. But also for the members of his church. Daily, minute by minute, people would roll through his mind, and he'd lift them up before the Lord. It was part of his job as pastor.

"Martin is out on the rodeo circuit anyway. Maybe we are the ones that are wrong, and their separate directions really are God's plan for their lives."

"Maybe." He definitely wasn't convinced of it.

"Well, unless God brings something to your mind, I'm fresh out of ideas. Although," she said, pausing to take a sip of her water, "our plans worked out beautifully with Ethan, and with Denver, and you really had a great plan with Crew and Burgundy. That Santa thing worked out better than I ever thought it would."

"Yeah. It was kind of hard for me to have the whole Santa thing in church, but it's the idea of giving, and Burgundy and Crew definitely benefited, as well as a bunch of other people in the church." He sighed. "Blakely and Martin took it over for a while, but it just didn't work out as well."

"They were already friends. They need a different kind of push," she said thoughtfully. "You know you did a good job with West too."

"Everyone could see that Poppy was perfect for him. He needed her."

"And man wasn't made to be alone," Penny said, a sentence both of them believed in strongly. The Bible was clear about that.

Race felt strongly that if God had taken the time to write them a handbook and give it to them, they should read it, study it, and use it to guide their lives.

Since God was quite capable of writing a book that was applicable down through the ages, being that He was God and He created the universe, Race always felt it was silly for anyone to pick and choose what he would and would not believe out of it.

It was an awful lot like the created telling the Creator he knew better than the Creator did.

Race figured after he created his first universe and a few planets, and maybe a person or two, then he would be qualified to start telling God what was best for him. Until that happened, he'd follow The Book.

He made a decision, picking up another piece of pizza from the box. They only splurged once in a while, and having another piece wasn't going to hurt anything. He watched as cheese strung out, thinning, as he lifted the slice and set it on his plate.

"Dante is coming to Mistletoe. He was gonna spend a month here anyway."

"But…" Penny looked at him, her brows drawn down in confusion. Blakely wasn't the girl that Dante was coming for. Dante didn't know that. And neither did the girl.

"No. I'm not thinking a match between Blakely and Dante. Goodness, that would never work. Even I can see that. But…"

It only took a second or two for his wife's eyes to widen and understanding to dawn across her face. "A decoy?"

"Exactly."

His wife nodded, smiling. "You're brilliant." She lifted her pizza and held it in front of her mouth. "Probably smart enough to be a brain surgeon."

He laughed. "I think I'll stick with hearts."

"You're definitely getting better."

A Gift from Jessie

View this code through your smart phone camera to be taken to a page where you can download a FREE ebook when you sign up to get updates from Jessie Gussman! Find out why people say, "Jessie's is the only newsletter I open and read" and "You make my day brighter. Love, love, love reading your newsletters. I don't know where you find time to write books. You are so busy living life. A true blessing." and "I know from now on that I can't be drinking my morning coffee while reading your newsletter – I laughed so hard I sprayed it out all over the table!"

Claim your free book from Jessie!

Escape to more faith-filled romance series by Jessie Gussman!

The Complete Sweet Water, North Dakota Reading Order:

Series One: Sweet Water Ranch Western Cowboy Romance (11 book series)

Series Two: Coming Home to North Dakota (12 book series)

Series Three: Flyboys of Sweet Briar Ranch in North Dakota (13 book series)

Series Four: Sweet View Ranch Western Cowboy Romance (10 book series)

Spinoffs and More! Additional Series You'll Love:

Jessie's First Series: Sweet Haven Farm (4 book series)

Small-Town Romance: The Baxter Boys (5 book series)

Bad-Boy Sweet Romance: Richmond Rebels Sweet Romance (3 book series)

Sweet Water Spinoff: Cowboy Crossing (9 book series)

Small Town Romantic Comedy: Good Grief, Idaho (5 book series)

True Stories from Jessie's Farm: Stories from Jessie Gussman's Newsletter (3 book series)

Reader-Favorite! Sweet Beach Romance: Blueberry Beach (8 book series)

Blueberry Beach Spinoff: Strawberry Sands (10 book series)

From Strawberry Sands to: Raspberry Ridge (12 book series)

Swoonfully Jolly Holiday Stories:

Holiday Romance: Cowboy Mountain Christmas (6 book series)

Cowboy Mountain Christmas Spinoff: A Heartland Cowboy Christmas (9 book series)

New and Much Loved: Mistletoe Meadows (4 books and counting!)

Laughing Through the Snow: Christmas Tree, PA Sweet Romcoms (6 short reads)